THE TOAD-THING

Cursing his loss, Conan reached beneath the temple's altar, meaning to sweep up the handful of jewels Zarono had left behind. Then he checked. The stone idol above the altar had begun to move! Its seven eyes, above the lipless mouth, fixed greenly on the Cimmerian; its stony limbs stretched and inched toward him.

'Crom!' A grunt of astonishment was torn from Conan.

The idol hunched and toppled from its pedestal, landing in the midst of the winking gems. Its four-fingered fore-limbs broke its fall, and without pause it advanced on him. It was toad-like but bulky as a buffalo, and Conan raised his cutlass in horror, knowing his steel could do naught against it ...

Also in the CONAN series from Sphere Books

Conan the Buccaneer

L. SPRAGUE DE CAMP and LIN CARTER

SPHERE SCIENCE FICTION AND FANTASY LIBRARY

SPHERE BOOKS LIMITED
London and Sydney

First published in Great Britain by Sphere Books Ltd 1975
30–32 Gray's Inn Road, London WC1X 8JL
Reprinted 1976 (three times), 1977, 1981, 1983, 1984, 1985

To the greatest living creator of swordsplay-
and-sorcery, J. R. R. Tolkein

Set in Linotype Baskerville

Printed and bound in Great Britain by
Cox & Wyman Ltd, Reading

CONTENTS

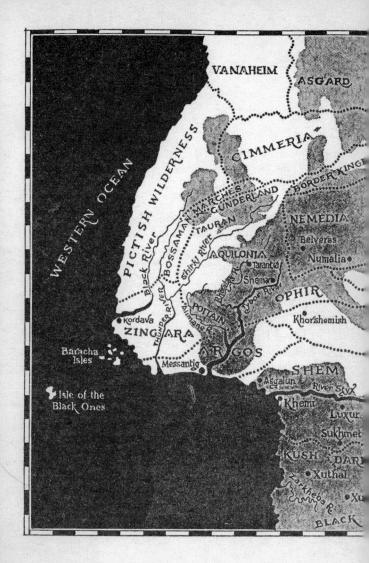

An Introduction by Lin Carter

BUCCANEERS AND BLACK MAGICIANS

THIS NOVEL is set in a world where there are no television talk shows, no income taxes, no commuter trains, no air pollution, no nuclear crises or campus riots or midi skirts.

A world blissfully innocent of detergent commercials, thirty-cent subway fares, Spiro T. Agnew speeches, freeze-dried coffee, electric toothbrushes, pornographic movies from Denmark, draft dodgers, Women's Lib, and the Los Angeles Freeway.

It is a world that never was but certainly should have been. A gorgeous, improbable, romantic world where all the men are handsome and heroic, all the girls impossibly beautiful and willing to dally back of the arena with a gladiator or two. A world made up of trackless jungles, mighty mountains, and shining seas, where cities blaze with barbaric splendor, glorious quests are possible, and adventure is a part of everyday life. It is crammed to the brim with weird monsters, sinister magicians, and grim-jawed warriors; a world where magic actually works and the gods exist in reality, not just in the imagination of their worshippers.

This is the world of a popular new kind of fiction we call Sword & Sorcery. Welcome it!

If you are one of those unfortunate few who have never before read a novel of Sword & Sorcery, you are in for a treat. A treat, that is, if you crave to escape for an hour or two from the above features of modern life into a gorgeous, impossible world. For Sword & Sorcery is sheer escapist reading, nothing more. It has no hidden meanings. It offers no handy, pre-packaged solution to any of the world's numerous ills. It has no 'ism' or 'ology' to sell, no message to put over. It is something remarkable and rare these days.

It is – *entertainment*.

These days, many people, including (alas!) many of my fellow science-fiction writers, seem to feel it is somehow vaguely immoral to read purely for pleasure. A story, say these wise men, should really come to grips with something crucial and important, like the oil slick on Laguna Beach, or the vanishing Yellowcrested Sandpiper. At very least, such persons advise, the hero should be a Negro striving to free his people, a homosexual gaily battling for social recognition, a concerned college youth protesting the iniquities of the Pentagon by blowing up his English Lit class, or an Amerindian getting back at the paleskins by seizing control of Alcatraz.

Social problems abound in modern fiction almost as much as on the front pages of our daily newspapers. And a novelist, they argue, should get out of his ivory tower and onto the barricades.

I disagree.

The world has been full of troubles since man climbed down from the trees and started inventing civilization. Social evils have flourished since the last Ice Age, at least. It is unlikely that my generation, or the next one, will solve any of the several ills that plague the body politic. Which is not to say that we should ignore them and pretend they are not there: but that we should see them in the context of history and realize that they are part of the human condition.

War, for example. There have always been wars, and few of them were fought for noble purposes. And crime. Crime in the streets is a large problem nowadays. But there has been crime in the streets going back to the day somebody invented streets. Just as there has been corruption in public office ever since the invention of public office, if not indeed before.

I see no reason why we should fill our every waking hour with brooding over the evils of the day. At least you will admit it is fun to lean back in a comfortable chair on a cold rainy evening, light a pipe, set a chill martini glass beside the ashtray, and escape into the pages of an extravagant romance, if only for an hour or two.

The urge to do this goes back at least to the days when old blind Homer sang of gallant warriors and cap-

10

tive beauties and isles of strange enchantment amid the unknown sea.

Technically speaking, we who practice the craft consider a tale to be Sword & Sorcery if it is a fast-moving and colorful adventure story laid in a preindustrial world where magic works and the gods are real – a tale which pits an heroic warrior in direct battle against the forces of supernatural evil.

Obviously, this is story-telling of a sort at least as old as Homer. Certainly the warrior hero battling evil monsters is a plot device that can be dated back to the Anglo-Saxon epic *Beowulf*, where the Geatish prince fought the ogre Grendel, or to the Germanic epic, the *Niebelungenleid*, in which Siegfried slew the dragon Fafnir.

This is quite true: the essential story elements that made up Sword & Sorcery are as old as literature itself.

But nobody writes much in the way of book-length epic poems these days. Hence it was only recently that these scattered and diverse story elements were reconstituted into what we call Sword & Sorcery.

The man who did this was a fiction writer for the adventure pulp magazines of the 1930s named Robert E. (for Ervin) Howard. Howard was born in 1906 in the town of Peaster, Texas, and spent most of his unhappily brief life in Cross Plains, which is deep in the heart of Texas between Brownwood and Abilene. He died there in 1936 when I was a little boy. I never knew him at all.

Howard was an adventure-story writer of the old school, nourished on the glorious tradition of Talbot Mundy, Harold Lamb, Edgar Rice Burroughs, and other pulpsters of the day. He really wanted to write pirate stories on the Spanish Main, or jungle yarns laid in darkest Africa, or tales of magic and mystery in unknown Tibet. But since he was attempting to break into the pages of Farnsworth Wright's *Weird Tales*, as his friends H. P. Lovecraft and Clark Ashton Smith were doing, he had to modify his natural bent toward fast-action yarns to include the elements of magic and supernatural horror.

His colleague and correspondent, Clark Ashton Smith, was then making it big in *Weird Tales* with cycles of stories laid against the exotic backgrounds of such lost civilizations of remotest antiquity as Hyperborea and Atlantis. These romantic and fabulous realms teemed with fantastic beasts of legend, with marvels and magicians and enigmatic gods and demons. Around much the same period his friend Lovecraft was selling stories of supernatural horror in which men of today faced and fought cosmic evil from beyond the stars. Good, entertaining stories, all of 'em, packed with thrills and shudders . . .

What Howard seems to have done is to incorporate all of these ideas into his own brand of rip-roaring adventure fiction. The result was a spectacularly successful series of superb stories about Conan the Cimmerian, a mighty warrior of barbarian lineage who went brawling and battling his way across the prehistoric world of legend, rising from such lowly professions as thief, bandit, pirate, and mercenary warrior, to a king's general and, eventually, to a throne of his own.

In pulling together the various elements of supernatural horror, ancient magic, and legendary prehistoric civilization, within the context of a fast-paced pulp adventure yarn, Howard contributed a new genre to the field of literature. We call it Sword & Sorcery.

Howard founded his private literary domain in 1932. In December of that year, *Weird Tales* published a story called 'The Phoenix on the Sword' under his byline. That was the first of all the Conan stories and it was an immediate sensation. The readers loved it and they clamored for more of the same. Howard happily settled down to creating his 'Hyborian Age' world and chronicling the adventures of its most celebrated citizen. He did not know he had only four years left to live.

In those four years he created a living, breathing legend. The readers ate up each Conan story as it appeared and clamored for more. Today, thirty-nine years later, they or their descendants are *still* clamoring for more; hence this novel by L. Sprague de Camp and myself.

Very few writers have the luck to create legends. Conan Doyle worked the trick with Sherlock Holmes, and Edgar Rice Burroughs did it with Tarzan of the Apes, and Ian Fleming may have pulled off the same miracle with

James Bond (it's too soon to tell, Bond-wise), but in only four years Robert Ervin Howard of Cross Plains, Texas, created a living legend that was not only to outlive its creator but also the magazine in which it first appeared and the publishing house which preserved it in the dignity of hard covers.

As was the case with Sherlock Holmes, Tarzan and even that newcomer to the ranks of the 'pop immortals', Commander James Bond of Her Majesty's Secret Service, other writers have not been able to keep their hands off Conan.

The first of the post-Howardians were content to merely imitate Howard's hero. Thus Henry Kuttner with his Elak of Atlantis yarns, and Kuttner's wife, C. L. Moore, with her Jirel of Joiry tales, and Norvell W. Page with his two short novels of Wan Tengri. Then other writers were inspired to work their own peculiar magic within much the same sort of world as that of Howard's Hyborian Age, but with more original characters – as Fritz Leiber with his magnificent saga of Fafhrd and the Gray Mouser, Michael Moorcock and his stories of Elric of Melnibone, the sinister, doomed albino princeling, or my collaborator, L. Sprague de Camp, with his deft, dry, witty tales of the Pusadian Age immediately following the collapse of Atlantis.

Sprague was a late convert to the Conan stories, while I had been reading them ever since my teens. The difference in our ages is considerable – he is my elder by twenty-three years – so it is somewhat surprising that I had read and loved Howard's stuff whole decades before he read a word of it. But, although a life-long devotee of fantastic fiction, Sprague got the impression from glimpses of the covers on the newsstand that *Weird Tales* consisted of ghost stories, a genre towards which he has always been able to restrain his enthusiasm. It was a reviewer's copy of the hard-cover edition of *Conan the Conqueror*, impulsively thrust upon him by his colleague Fletcher Pratt, that introduced Sprague to Sword & Sorcery. Once off, there was no stopping him: he became an avid enthusiast and, when he discovered that unpublished and, in some cases, unfinished Conan stories existed in manuscript caches scattered around the country, he began tracking them down, completing and revising them, and getting them into print, with the assistance of Howard's agent Glenn Lord.

In the meanwhile I had grown up out of my teens, spent a tour of duty with the infantry in Korea, and moved to New York to take some writing workshop courses at Columbia University. In 1965 I began selling novels to the paperbacks, beginning with a book called *The Wizard of Lemuria*, which has been described, rather charitably, as 'the result of a head-on collision between Howard and Burrough'.

My first Lemurian novel became the start of a series of six, and besides these tales of Thongor the Mighty, barbarian warrior-king of Lost Lemuria, I have written six or seven other novels of Sword & Sorcery.

Our mutual enthusiasm for fantasy in general and heroic fantasy in particular brought Sprague and me together at many science-fiction conventions and through the medium of a casual correspondence. Then in 1967 I edited and completed a book of Howard's stories called *King Kull*, which consisted of an abortive pre-Conan series of Sword & Sorcery narratives about an Atlantean savage named Kull.

The volume was published by Lancer Books and is, I believe, still in print. Lancer, at Sprague's urging, had begun issuing its history-making series of Conan books, as edited, arranged, and completed by L. Sprague de Camp. That same year Sprague invited me to collaborate with him on 'some new Conan stories to help fill up the larger gaps between the extant tales'. We have been doing so ever since.

Collaboration with L. Sprague de Camp has been and continues to be a fascinating experience and a vast pleasure (I was reading L. Sprague de Camp back in my teens, too). It is very interesting to learn at first hand how his mind works and how he thinks out a story. I like to think I have learned something about my craft from observing him at work, for he is one of the greatest living masters of that craft, and the education I have received during this collaboration has been unique.

This novel of buccaneers and black magicians is, according to the internal sequence of the saga, the sixth volume

14

in order of our outline of Conan's life and career. The story serves to cover an otherwise inadequately chronicled period of Conan's biography, those two years in which he was a buccaneer of Zingara. We have used this book to strengthen the internal connections of the saga, too: herein first appears that same bluff, hearty Vanr, Sigurd, who reappears in the twelfth and last book, *Conan of the Isles;* here, too, reappears one of Conan's old comrades, that stalwart black warrior, Juma of Kush, who first appeared on stage in the story 'The City of Skulls', in the first book of the saga, called *Conan.* We have further tightened the internal logic of the saga as a whole by presenting here the character of Zarono for his first appearance in the series (he makes a comeback in the story 'The Treasure of Tranicos' in the eighth volume, *Conan the Usurper*), and by using for our chief villain the magnificent Prince of Magicians, Thoth-Amon of Stygia, who frequently makes an appearance throughout the saga as a whole. Conan, incidentally, is about thirty-seven or thirty-eight at this point in the saga.

As my collaborator and I see this novel, *Conan the Buccaneer,* through press, it is not without a certain nostalgia. We have only one more Conan book to write and the series will be at last finished. The saga of the mighty Cimmerian, whose first appearance in print was almost forty years ago, will come to a close with *Conan of Aquilonia.*

Howard lived to see eighteen of his Conan stories printed. Eight others, ranging all the way from completed manuscripts to mere fragments or outlines, have since been discovered among his papers. The team of de Camp and Carter have added eight more stories to that total, two of them book-length novels, not including a couple of oddities such as 'The Hand of Nergal' (by Howard and Carter) and 'The Snout in the Dark, (by Howard, de Camp, *and* Carter). All things considered, Sprague (variously working in collaboration with Howard, myself, and Bjorn Nyberg) has probably added more wordage to the Conan saga than Howard wrote originally.

But the end, as I say, is at last in sight.

Not the end of Conan himself, of course.

He will go on for many years to come. These books will no doubt continue in print for years . . . perhaps longer than seems likely right now.

Besides mere books, Conan has now become a comic-book hero with a magazine all of his own (see your news-stand for Marvel's *Conan the Barbarian*).

And, from time to time, it looks as if Hollywood might discover the doughty and durable Cimmerian. We were in negotiation with one producer for a solid year there for a time. Other nibbles have come from the movie folk. More doubtless lurk in the unseen corridors of the future.

And the readers are still clamoring for more . . .

LIN CARTER
Hollis, Long Island, New York

Prologue

DREAM OF BLOOD

Two HOURS before midnight, the princess Chabela awoke. Drawing the filmy coverlet about her naked body, the buxom daughter of King Ferdrugo of Zingara lay tense and trembling. She stared into the darkness, while cold horror sent thrills of premonition through her quickening nerves. Outside, rain drummed on the palace roofs.

What had it been about, that dark and dreadful dream from whose shadowy clutches her soul had so barely escaped?

Now that the ghastly dream was over, she could hardly recall its details. There had been darkness, and evil eyes glaring through the murk; the glitter of knives – and blood. Blood everywhere: on the sheets, on the tiled floor, crawling beneath the door – red, sticky, sluggishly flowing blood!

Shuddering, Chabela tore her thoughts from this morbid introspection. The glimmer of a night light caught her glance; it came from a waxen taper in a sconce on the low, ornate prie-dieu across the chamber. On the prie-dieu also stood a small painted icon of Mitra, Lord of Light and chief divinity of the Kordavan pantheon. An impulse to seek supernatural guidance brought her to stand shivering on the tiles. Wrapping the lacy coverlet about her voluptuous, olive-hued body, she crossed the bedchamber to kneel before the idol. Her night-black torrent of hair poured down her back like a cataract of a liquid midnight.

Atop the prie-dieu stood a small silver canister of incense. She uncapped it and tossed a few grains of the gummy powder into the flickering flame. The rich odor of nard and myrrh filled the air.

Chabela clasped her hands and bowed as if to pray, but no words came. Her mind was a jumble. Strive as she would, she could not attain the serene inner control required for effective divine supplication.

17

It came to her that, for many days, shadowy terrors had lurked in the palace. The old king had seemed distant, distraught, preoccupied with unknown problems. He had aged astoundingly, as if his vitality were being sucked away by some phantasmal leech. Some of his decrets had been unlike him, at variance with the tenor of his previous reign. There were times when another person's spirit seemed to peer through his faded old eyes, to speak with his slow, harsh voice, or to scrawl a wavering signature on documents that he had dictated. The thought was absurd, but it was there.

And then, these terrible dreams of knives and blood and staring eyes; of thickening, watchful shadows that peered and whispered!

Abruptly, her mind cleared as if a fresh wind from the sea had blown a mist away from her consciousness. She found she could name the feeling of haunting dread that oppressed her. It was as if some dark force had striven to seize control of her very mind.

Horror filled her; a sob of loathing shook her rounded body. Her full young breasts, proud globes of pale tan under lacy veils, rose and fell. She threw herself prone before the little altar, her black hair sliding in gleaming coils over the tiles. She prayed:

'Lord Mitra, defender of the House of Ramiro, champion of mercy and justice, chastiser of depravity and cruelty, help me, I beg thee, in my hour of need! Tell me what to do, I beseech thee, mighty Lord of Light!'

Rising, she opened the golden box beside the canister on the prie-dieu and drew forth a dozen slim rods of carven sandalwood. Some of these divining straws were short, some long; some were branched or crooked, others straight and plain.

She threw them down at random on the floor before the altar. The clatter of the slender sticks was loud in the silence.

She peered down at the jumble of fallen rods, the black bell of her hair framing her young face. Her eyes rounded with awe.

The sticks spelled T-O-V-A-R-R-O.

The girl repeated the name. 'Tovarro,' she said slowly. 'Go to Tovarro . . .' Determination flashed in her dark

18

eyes. 'I will!' she vowed. 'Tonight! I'll rout out Captain Kapellez ...'

As she moved about the chamber, flashes of lightning from the storm outside intermittently lighted the scene. She snatched garments from a chest. She gathered up a baldric with a scabbarded rapier and collected a warm cloak. She glided about the boudoir with a swift economy of motion.

From the prie-dieu, Mitra watched with glassy eyes. Was there a faint glitter of ghostly intelligence in the painted gaze? And a slight expression of stern pity on those sculptured lips? Was the rumble of distant thunder his voice? None could say.

Within the hour, however, Ferdrugo's daughter was gone from the palace. Thus was set in motion a sequence of fantastic events, which would bring a·mighty warrior, a dreaded sorcerer, a proud princess, and ancient gods into a weird confrontation on the edge of the known world.

Chapter 1

AN OLD ZINGARAN CUSTOM

THE WIND had been rising, whipping gusts of rain before it. Now, after midnight, the damp sea wind howled through the cobbled alleys that led away from the harbor. It swung the painted wooden signs above the doors of inns and taverns. Starved mongrels cowered, shivering, in doorways against the wind and rain.

At this late hour, the revelers were done. Few lights burned in the houses of Kordava, capital of Zingara on the Western Ocean. Heavy clouds obscured the moon, and tattered rags of vapor scudded across the gloomy sky like ghosts. It was a dark, secretive hour – the time of night when hard-eyed men whisper of treason and robbery; when masked assassins slink through nighted chambers, envenomed daggers bright in their black-gloved hands. A night for conspiracy; a night for murder.

A tramp of feet and the occasional clink of a sword in its scabbard made itself heard above the sounds of wind and rain. A detachment of the night watch – six men, booted and cloaked, with hat brims pulled low against the weather and with pikes and halberds on shoulder – strode through the nighted streets. They made little noise, save an occasional low-voiced remark in the liquid Zingaran tongue. They glanced right and left sharply for signs of doors or windows feloniously forced; they listened for sounds of disturbance; they tramped on, thinking of the flagons of wine they would down, once their dank patrol was over.

After the watch had passed an abandoned stable with its roof half fallen in, two shadowy figures, who had been standing motionless inside, came to life. From beneath his cloak, one produced a small dark lantern and uncovered its bull's eye. The beam of the candle inside the lantern picked out a spot on the stable floor.

Stooping, the man with the lantern brushed dirt away and uncovered a stone trapdoor, to which was stapled a short length of chain ending in a bronze ring. Both

20

men seized the ring and heaved. The trapdoor rose with a squeak of unoiled hinges. The two dark figures disappeared into the aperture, and the trapdoor returned with a thump to its former position.

A narrow stone stair spiraled down into darkness, feebly broken by the wavering beam of the dark lantern. Old and worn were the stones of this stair; mold and fungus beslimed the rounded steps. The must of centuries of decay wafted up the shaft.

The two black-cloaked men descended the stair with cautious, silent steps. Silken masks concealed their features. Like shadowy specters, they felt their way downward, while a wet sea breeze from the passageways below – secret tunnels connected with the open sea – stirred their cloaks and raised them like the wings of giant bats.

High above the sleeping town, the towers of the castle of Villagro, duke of Kordava, soared against the somber sky. Few lights burned in the tall, slitted windows, for few of the dwellers were awake.

Far beneath this pile of ancient masonry, however, a man sat studying parchments by the light of a tall golden candelabrum, whose branches bore the likeness of intertwined serpents.

No cost had been spared to render the stony vault a seat of luxury. Walls of damp, rough stone were hung with richly embroidered tapestries. The cold stone flags of the floor were hidden by a thick, soft carpet of many colors – scarlet, gold, emerald, azure, and violet – in the complex, florid designs of distant Vendhya.

A taboret of gilded wood, decorated with subtly sensuous groupings of meticulously detailed nude figures in carved relief, bore a silver tray laden with refreshments: wine of Kyros in a crystal decanter, fruit and pastries in silver bowls.

The desk, whereat the man sat reading, was huge and ornately carved after the style of imperial Aquilonia to the northeast. An inkwell of gold and crystal held a peacock plume for a quill. A slender sword lay across the desk like a paperweight.

The man himself was of middle years, perhaps fifty, but lean and elegant. His slender legs were clad in black silken hose and graceful shoes of the beautifully tooled

21

leather of Kordava, with gemmed buckles, which flashed as he impatiently tapped his toe. His wiry torso was clad in a doublet of turquoise velvet, the sleeves of which were puffed and slashed to display an inner lining of peach-colored satin. Snowy lace foamed at his lean wrists. A huge jewel gleamed on each finger of his carefully-groomed hands.

The man's age was revealed by the sagging flesh of his jowls and the dark, baggy circles beneath his cold, quick, dark eyes. He had obviously tried to hide his years, for the hair that was smoothly combed to his shoulders was dyed, and a veneer of powder softened the lines in his aristocratic features. But the cosmetics failed to conceal the roughened flesh, the discolorations beneath the hard, weary eyes, and the wattled neck.

With one bejewelled hand, he played with the parchments – official documents with gilt and crimson seals and fluttering ribbons, inscribed with ornate cursive penmanship. The man's tapping toe and the frequent glances at the handsome water clock on the sideboard betrayed his impatience. He also sent his dark glance toward a heavy arras in the corner.

Behind the man at the desk, a silent Kushite slave stood with heavily muscled arms folded upon his naked chest. Golden hoops flashed in his elongated earlobes; the candlelight shone on the musculature of his splendid torso. A naked scimitar was thrust through a crimson sash.

With a clashing of tiny gears, the water clock chimed. It was two hours past midnight.

With a muffled curse, the man at the desk threw down the crackling parchment he had been studying. At that instant, the arras was drawn aside, disclosing the mouth of a secret passage. Two men, cloaked and masked in black, stood in the mouth of the passage. One bore a small lantern; the light of the candelabrum sparkled on the intruders' wet cloaks.

The seated man had set one hand on the hilt of the rapier that lay across the desk, while the Kushite seized the scimitar at his waist. As the two men entered the chamber and doffed their masks, however, the older man relaxed.

'It's all right, Gomani,' he said to the black, who

22

again folded his arms on his chest and resumed his indifferent stare.

The two newcomers dropped their cloaks to form shapeless black heaps on the floor and bowed to him at the desk. The first man, tossing back the cowl of his robe to disclose a bald or shaven skull, hawknosed features, aloof black eyes, and a thin mouth, clasped his hands before his breast and bowed over them.

The other man set down his lantern and made a leg with courtly grace, doffing his plumed hat in a low bow and murmuring 'My lord Duke!' When he rose again to stand nonchalantly with one hand on the jeweled hilt of a long sword, it could be seen that he was a tall, slender, black-haired man with sallow skin and a sharp-featured, predatory face. His thin black mustachios were so precise that they might have been added to his face by an artist. He had a flavor of spurious gentility: a touch of theatrical flamboyance and more than a touch of the piratical.

Villagro, duke of Kordava, fixed the gaunt Zingaran with an icy glance. 'Master Zarono, I am not accustomed to being kept waiting,' he observed.

Again that courtly bow. 'A thousand pardons, Your Grace! Not for the blessings of all the gods would I have displeased you.'

'Then why are you half an hour late, sirrah?'

A graceful gesture. 'A mere nothing – a wisp of foolery—'

The man with the priestly shaven skull put in: 'A tavern brawl, lord Duke.'

'A brawl in a common wineshop?' demanded the duke. 'Have you lost your wits, you scoundrel? How did this happen?'

His sallow cheeks flushing, Zarono cast a glare of menace at the priest, who returned his look impassively. ''Twas naught, Your Grace! Nothing that need detain you—'

'I will judge that, Zarono,' said the duke. 'It is not impossible that our plan has been bertayed. Are you certain that this – ah – interruption was not a provocation?' The duke's hands closed on a folded letter and tightened until their knuckles whitened.

Zarono gave a smooth little laugh. 'Nothing at all like

that, my lord. Perhaps you have heard of an oafish barbarian called Conan, who has risen to command of a Zingaran privateer, notwithstanding that he is but the whelp of some Cimmerian slut in the frozen North?'

'I know nothing of the rogue. Continue.'

'As I say, 'twas naught. But, entering the Inn of the Nine Drawn Swords for my rendezvous with the holy Menkara here, I espied a roast sizzling on the spit and, as I had not replenished nature since dawn, I resolved to slay two pigeons with a single bolt. Since a man of my quality cannot be expected to waste his time in waiting, I hailed Sabral the taverner and commanded him to set the haunch before me. Then this Cimmerian lout, claiming it was his dinner, dared oppose me. A gentleman can scarce be expected to brook that upstart outlanders be given preference—'

'What happened? Come to the point,' said the duke.

'There was some argument, and from words we passed to buffets.' Zarono chuckled as he touched a dark swelling beneath one eye. 'The fellow is strong as a bull, although I flatter myself that I also marked his ugly visage. Before I could show the peasant the temper of my steel, the taverner and some of his customers seized us and forced us apart – not without effort, as it took four or five of them to hold either of us. In the meantime, the holy father Menkara here had arrived, and he devoted himself to assuaging our angry passions. What with one thing and another . . .'

'I see; it was in all probability a mere accident. But you should know better than to provoke such broils. I will not have it! And now to business. This, I presume, is . . . ?'

The Zingaran twirled his mustachios. 'Pardon my ill manners, Your Grace; I present the holy Menkara, a priest of Set, whom I have persuaded to join our high emprise and who now labors diligently in the cause.'

The shaven-headed one again clasped hands and bowed. Villagro nodded curtly.

'Why did you insist on a personal interview, holy Father?' he snapped. 'I prefer to work through agents like Zarono. Is aught amiss? Is the compensation offered you enough?'

The glazed eyes of the bald Stygian bore a deceptive

look of dull indifference. 'Gold is but dross; yet, for all that, the fleshly envelope must be sustained on this lowly plane of being. Our cultus knows that the world is but an illusion – a mask over the naked face of chaos . . . But pardon this lowly one, lord Duke. Theological discourse is a custom of my land, but my presence here is due to the custom of your country, eh?' The Stygian gave a bleak little smile, indicating that he had made a joke.

Duke Villagro raised an inquiring eyebrow. Menkara continued: 'I refer to Your Grace's plan to compel the amiable but senile King Ferdrugo to bestow the hand of Princess Chabela upon you, before the well-timed end of his existence on this planet. I alluded to the well-known apothegm: "Conspiracy and treason are venerable customs in Zingara."'

Villagro's grimace showed that he did not deem the joke very humorous. 'Yes, yes, priest, all this we know. What is your news? How goeth the struggle to capture our subjects' minds?'

The Stygian shrugged. 'All goeth poorly, my lord. The mind of Ferdrugo is easily dominated, for he is old and sickly. I have, however, encountered a problem.'

'Well?'

'When I have the king under the valence of my will, I can command him perfectly. I can force him to give you the princess's hand; but the princess – not unreasonably, given the difference in your ages – balks.'

'Then place her mind under your control as well, you bald-pated fool!' snarled Villagro, irked by the allusion to his age.

Cold fires flared in the Stygian's dull eyes but were swiftly banked. 'This very night have I striven to that end,' he purred. 'My spirit came upon the princess slumbering in her suite and intruded into her dreams. She is young, strong, and vital. With the greatest difficulty, I achieved control of her brain – but even as my shadow whispered to her sleeping soul, I felt my control over the old king's mind loosen and slip away. I swiftly released the girl to reassume my mastery of her father. She awoke in terror and, although she remembers naught of my whispered suggestions, I have doubtless alarmed her.

'Here is the problem. I cannot at the same time control both king and princess—'

He broke off, for fire blazed up in the duke's eyes. 'So it was you, you bungling dog!' roared Villagro.

Surprise and alarm flickered in the Stygian's dull gaze. 'What means my lord?' he murmured. Zarono added his query to that of the priest.

The duke voiced a strangled oath. 'Is it possible that my cunning spy and my canny sorcerer are oblivious to what has half the city in a buzz?' he shouted. 'Can it be that neither of you idiots know that the princess has disappeared from the city? And that all our plans are set at naught?'

Duke Villagro had laid his plans with care. King Ferdrugo was decrepit and ailing. To insure a peaceful succession, the royal princess, Chabela, must soon wed. Who could better sue for her hand and follow her to the throne than Villagro, a widower of many years and, after the king, the richest and most powerful peer of the realm?

In the crypt beneath his ancient castle, Villagro had advanced his scheme. The privateer Zarono, of noble lineage but tarnished past, he enlisted in his cause. To Zarono he gave the task of enlisting a sorcerer of flexible scruples, who could influence the mind and will of the aging monarch. For this mission, the wily Zarono had selected Menkara, wizard-priest of the outlawed Stygian cult of Set. Chabela's flight, however, threw all Villagro's plans awry. What booted it to control the mind of the king if the princess were no longer present to be wedded?

With stony self-possession, Menkara gradually calmed the agitated Villagro. He said: 'May it please Your Grace, but such modest mastery of the occult sciences as I possess should soon reveal the lady's present location.'

'Do it, then,' said Villagro gloomily.

At the priest's direction, Gomani the Kushite fetched a bronze tripod and charcoal from the adjacent torture cell. The carpet was rolled back, revealing the stony pave. From beneath his robe, the Stygian produced a large wallet with many interior compartments. From this he took a piece of luminous green chalk, with which he traced on the floor a circular design like a serpent holding its tail in its jaws.

Meanwhile, the Kushite kindled a small fire on the tripod. Blowing and fanning soon raised the charcoal to red heat.

On the glowing coals, the priest poured a fragrant green fluid from a crystal phial. With a serpentine hiss, a sharp aromatic odor filled the still air of the chamber. Pale-green spirals of smoke coiled and writhed in the drowsy air.

The priest seated himself tailor-fashion in the circle of green chalk. The candelabrum was extinguished, plunging the chamber into an eery gloom. Three sources of light remained: the red glow of the coals in the brazier, the green-glowing serpentiform circle of chalk, and the yellow eyes of the sorcerer, which blazed like the orbs of some nocturnal beast.

The voice of the Stygian rose, chanting: 'Iao, Setesh . . . Setesh, Iao! Abrathax kuraim mizraeth, Setesh!'

The harsh, sibilant words died to a droning whisper, then faded away. The only sound was that of the slow rhythm of the Stygian's breathing. As he sank into a trance, his yellow orbs were veiled by his eyelids.

'Mitra!' gasped Zarono, but the vise-like grip of the duke on his arm enjoined him to silence.

The coils of smoke writhed and diffused into a luminous, jade-green cloud. Patches of light and dark appeared in the vapor. Then the watchers gazed upon a life-like scene within the cloud. This scent showed a small ship, caravel-rigged, racing across a nighted sea. On the foredeck stood a young girl, her rounded form apparent through the heavy cloak, which the wind whipped tightly against her vigorous young body . . .

'Chabela!' breathed Villagro.

As if his murmur broke the spell, the glowing cloud eddied and fragmented. The coals went out with a hiss. The priest fell forward, his bald brow thudding against the floor.

'Whither is she bound?' Villagro asked Menkara when a swallow of wine had revived the sorcerer.

The Stygian pondered. 'I read the name of Asgalun

in her mind. Know you of any reason why she should seek Asgalun, Your Grace?'

'That is where the king's brother, Tovarro, has his present seat,' mused the duke. 'As ambassador, he roves from one Shemite city to another, but that is where he now is. I see it! She will flee to Tovarro and beseech him to return to Kordava. With that meddlesome fellow here, the gods only know what would befall our plans. Well, then, what's to do, since your powers cannot dominate both king and princess simultaneously?'

Zarono stretched out a hand toward the silver tray, murmuring: 'With Your Grace's kind permission?' At Villagro's nod, Zarono helped himself to a piece of fruit. 'Methinks,' he said between bites, 'we should get another sorcerer.'

'That makes good sense,' said the duke. 'Whom do you suggest, priest?'

The Stygian brooded without expression. 'The chief of my order,' he said at last, 'and the mightiest magician now carnate on this plane, is the great Thoth-Amon.'

'Where does this Thoth-Ammon reside?'

'He dwells in his native Stygia, in the Oasis of Khajar,' replied Menkara. 'I must, however, warn Your Grace that the mighty talents of Thoth-Amon are not to be purchased with mere gold.' A bitter smile curled the swarthy lips. 'Gold can buy little men, like me; but Thoth-Amon is a veritable prince of sorcery. One who commands the spirits of the earth has no need of material wealth.'

'What, then, can tempt him?'

'One dream lies close to Thoth-Amon's heart,' purred the priest. 'Centuries ago, the cults of the accursed Mitra and of my own divinity, Set, warred here in these western realms. Such were the twists of fate that my cultus was thrown down, while the Mitra-worshipers were exalted over us. The worship of the Serpent was outlawed, and all of my order were driven into exile.

'Now, if Your Grace would swear to throw down the temples of Mitra and rebuild the fanes of Set in their place, and elevate great Set over the upstart gods of the West, then I daresay that Thoth-Amon would lend his power to your schemes.'

The duke chewed his lip. Gods, temples, and priests

28

meant nothing to him, so long as the temples and their hierarchy paid their taxes. He shrugged.

'It shall be so,' he said. 'I will swear it by any gods or demons your wonder-worker names. Now, here are your tasks:

'At dawn, you shall put to sea. Set your course to the southeast and intercept the vessel bearing the princess. Seize her and destroy the ship, leaving no survivors to tell the tale. Your *Petrel*, Zarono, should easily overhaul the little *Sea Queen*.

'Having secured the lady, you shall continue on to Stygia. You, Menkara, shall guide the party to Thoth-Amon's stronghold and serve as my ambassador to him. When you have enlisted him in our cause, you shall return to Kordava with him and the princess. Are there any questions?'

Thus the double mission was launched.

Chapter 2

A KNIFE IN THE DARK

DAWN PALED the eastern sky. The storm had blown over. Now broken, black clouds scudded across the somber heavens. A few faint stars, lingering in the west, were seen intermittently through the gaps in the clouds and were reflected in the puddles of muddy rainwater in the gutters of Kordava.

Zarono, master of the privateer *Petrel* and secret agent of the duke of Kordava, strode through the wet streets in a foul mood. His exchange of fisticuffs with the giant Cimmerian buccaneer had not sweetened his temper, to say nothing of his having missed his dinner. The imprecations heaped upon him by his master the duke had further soured his disposition, and to top it all he was bleary-eyed with lack of sleep and ravenously hungry. As he dodged dripping eaves and hiked the edges of his cloak out of muddy puddles, his mouth tasted of smothered anger. He yearned for something helpless on which to vent his wrath. Menkara loped silently at his side.

A scrawny little man, whose bare legs could be seen under the ragged hem of his patched cassock, strove to keep his footing on the greasy cobbles as he scurried through the gusty streets. His sandals slapped against the wet stones. With one hand he gathered a patched shawl about his meager chest; with the other he held aloft a burning link of tarred rope to light his way.

Under his breath, he mumbled the dawn litany to Mitra. To him, this was a mere jumble of meaningless sounds, for his mind was elsewhere. Thus Ninus, a minor priest of the Mitraic temple, hurried through the wet, windy streets to his destiny.

Ninus had risen from his pallet before dawn and, eluding the preceptor, had crept from the precincts of the temple of Mitra into a gloom-drenched alley. Thence he made his way toward the harbor of Kordava and his meeting with the foreign corsair, Conan the Cimmerian.

The unprepossessing little man had a wobbling paunch and spindly shanks. Watery eyes looked out over a huge nose. He was wrapped in a tattered robe of the Mitraic priesthood – a robe that was none too clean and suspiciously stained with the purple spots of forbidden wine. In his earlier years, before seeing the light of Mitra, Ninus had been one of the ablest jewel thieves of the Hyborian lands; this was how he had become acquainted with Conan. Never much of a temple goer, the burly privateer had also once been a thief himself, and the two were friends of long standing. Although Ninus felt that his call to the priesthood was sincere, he had never succeeded in subduing the fleshly appetites that he had so freely indulged in his former life.

Close to his scrawny bosom, the little priest hugged the document that Conan had promised to buy. The privateer needed treasure, and Ninus required gold – or at least silver. The chart had long been in Ninus' possession. In his thieving days, the little man had often thought of following its inked path to the fabulous wealth whose hiding place it professed to disclose. But since, in his present holy profession, it seemed unlikely that he would ever hunt treasure again, why not sell the map?

His mind full of rosy visions of sweet wine, hearty roasts, and plump wenches that, he hoped, Conan's money would obtain, Ninus scurried around the corner – and ran full into two men in dark cloaks, who stepped aside to avoid him. Murmuring an apology, the little priest peered near-sightedly at the gaunt man whose hooded robes had fallen back. Then astonishment shocked him out of his normal prudence.

'Menkara the Setite!' he cried shrilly. 'You here? Vile snake-worshiper, how dare you?' Raising his voice in righteous wrath, Ninus shouted for the watch.

Growling an oath, Zarono seized his companion to hurry him away, but the Stygian tore loose and turned blazing eyes upon him. 'The little swine knows me!' he hissed. 'Slay him quickly, else we are all undone!'

Zarono hesitated but an instant, then whipped out his dagger and thrust. The life of one miserable priest meant nothing to him; the important thing was not to have to answer the questions of the watch.

The gleam of the steel blade in the waxing light of dawn was quenched in the robes of the Mitraist. Ninus staggered back with a choking cry, gasped, and crumpled up on the cobbles. A drop of blood oozed from his mouth.

The Stygian spat. 'So perish all your abominable kind!' he snarled.

Peering nervously about, Zarono hastily wiped his blade clean on the fallen man's cloak. 'Let us begone!' he growled.

But the Stygian's eyes had noticed a bulge in Ninus' tunic. He crouched and took a small roll of parchment from the Mitraist's garment. With both hands, he spread the document.

'A chart of some kind,' mused the sorcerer. 'With study, methinks I could decipher—'

'Later, later!' insisted Zarono. 'Hasten, ere the watch find us!'

Menkara nodded and secreted the scroll. The two men slunk off through the reddening mists of dawn, leaving Ninus sprawled on the cobbles.

Fed by poor wine, an inconclusive scuffle with the sneering Zarono, and hours of idle waiting, Conan's humor had grown steadily worse. Now, restless as a jungle cat, he prowled the common room of the smoky inn, whose ceiling barely cleared the top of his head. Although the Nine Drawn Swords had earlier been crowded, there were now only a few customers left, such as a trio of drunken seamen sprawled in the corner. Two of these softly sang chantey's off key and out of time, while the third had fallen asleep.

The time candle told Conan that dawn was approaching. Ninus was hours overdue. Something must have befallen the little priest, who would never be so late when there was money to be had. Speaking Zingaran with a barbarous accent, Conan growled to the stout taverner:

'Sabral!' I'm going out for a breath of fresh air. If any ask for me, I shall be back soon.'

Outside, the rain had died to mere eaves-dripping. The black blanket of cloud had broken up and rolled away. The silver moon again peered forth, to illumine

32

the last of the night; but already she had paled in the growing light of dawn. Wisps of mist arose from the puddles.

With a hearty belch, Conan strode heavily along the wet cobbles, meaning to take a turn around the block in which the Nine Drawn Swords stood. He cursed Ninus under his breath. The holy little tosspot would make him lose the dawn breeze, which would carry the *Wastrel* out of the harbor of Kordava. Without it, they might have to put the longboat over and warp the ship out by laborious towing.

Then Conan suddenly halted, frozen motionless. Huddled in the rain-streaming gutter, a shapeless clump of soiled garments and sprawled limbs had caught his gaze.

His eyes probed right and left, searching housetops, doorways, and the mouths of alleys for signs of lurking assailants. Gently he brushed aside his heavy black rain cloak and eased the cutlass in his scabbard. In this quarter of the old city, a corpse was no cause for surprise. The crumbling hovels that lined the crooked alleys harbored thieves, assassins, and other such human scum. But where a victim lies, his assailant sometimes lurks nearby, and Conan had long since learned caution in such matters.

As silently as a prowling leopard, the burly Cimmerian slunk through the shadows to kneel beside the huddled figure. With one careful hand he turned it over on its back. Fresh blood glittered darkly in the reddening light of dawn. The cowl fell back to reveal the face.

'Crom!' growled Conan. For this was the ex-thief and priest, Ninus of Messantia, for whom Conan had waited so long.

With swift hands, the Cimmerian examined the body. The chart, which Ninus had promised to bring to the inn to sell him, was missing.

As Conan squatted back on his haunches, his thoughts raced swiftly behind his grim, impassive features. Who would wish the death of an insignificant little priestling, with no more than a few coppers in his purse? The chart was the only thing of any value that the priest could have carried. Since it was absent, logic asserted that the harmless Ninus must have been knifed so that his assailant could possess himself of the chart.

The upper limb of the rising sun reddened the towers and roof ridges of old Kordava. In its light, Conan's volcanic gaze burst into fierce blue flame. Clenching his scarred fist, the giant Cimmerian swore that someone should pay for this deed, and in blood.

Gently, the Cimmerian lifted the small body in his powerful arms and strode swiftly back to the Nine Drawn Swords. Pushing into the common room, he barked at the taverner:

'Sabral! A private room and a chirurgeon, and quickly!'

The taverner knew that, when he used this tone, the Cimmerian brooked no delay. He hastened to lead Conan with his burden up the rickety stairs to the second floor.

The eyes of the few remaining customers followed the Cimmerian's course with curious stares. They saw a tall man, almost a giant, of enormously powerful build. The dark, scarred face under the battered sailor's hat was clean-shaven, and the heavy, sun-bronzed features were framed by a square-cut mane of coarse black hair. The deep-set eyes under the massive black brows were blue. The buccaneer carried the body in his arms with as little effort as if it had been a small child.

None of Conan's crew was in the tavern. Conan had made sure of this when he had formed his appointment with Ninus, for he did not wish news of the treasure chart to pass current among the crew until he was ready to tell them himself.

Sabral led Conan to the chamber that he reserved for guests of quality. Conan started to lay Ninus on the bed, but he paused as Sabral whisked the bedspread out from under the body.

'No blood on my best spread!' he said.

'Fiends take your spread!' snarled Conan, laying Ninus down. While Sabral folded the spread, Conan examined Ninus. The priest breathed faintly, and his pulse fluttered.

'He lives, at least,' growled Conan. 'Get you gone,

34

man, and fetch a leech! Do not stand gaping like an idiot!'

The taverner silently vanished. Conan bared Ninus' torso and crudely bound the wound, which still seeped blood.

Sabral entered with a yawning physician in a night robe, with a straggle of gray hairs escaping from under the edges of his nightcap.

'The good Doctor Cratos,' said the taverner.

The physician undid Conan's bandage, cleansed the wound, and bound it up again with a clean cloth. 'Luckily,' said he, 'the stab seems to have missed the heart and the large blood vessels and to have only scratched the lung. With good care, he should live. Are you paying for him, Captain?'

Conan grunted assent. A few swallows of wine restored Ninus to partial consciousness. In a voice that was little more than a whisper, the priest told his tale:

'I ran into – two men – on the street. One – Menkara, the priest of Set. I cried – cried out. He told – the other – slay me.'

'Who was the other?' demanded Conan.

'All wrapped up – wide hat and cloak – but methinks – buccaneer Zarono . . .'

Conan scowled. Zarono! That was the sneering privateer with whom he had quarreled, hours before. Had Zarono heard of his rendezvous with Ninus and waylaid the priest to rob him of the chart? Everything pointed to a shrewd conspiracy to wrest the secret of the treasure from Conan.

He stood up, his face flushed with anger. 'Here!' he rumbled. Digging a fistful of coins from his purse, he slapped them into Cratos' palm. Another handful was pressed upon Sabral.

'See that he has good care and gets well, you two!' said Conan. 'We'll settle the exact charges when I return, and woe betide you if you do not your best for him! If he dies, bury him with the full rites of Mitra. Now I'm off.'

Like a ghost, he vanished out the door of the chamber, glided down the stair, and plunged out the heavy front door of the Inn of the Nine Drawn Swords. He strode swiftly, with the heavy black cloak flapping about his boot heels.

As the risen sun gilded the masts and yards of the ships, the harbor bustled with activity. Sailors scrambled up and down the rigging, officers bellowed commands through parchment speaking trumpets, and creaking wooden cranes, powered by the muscles of longshoremen straining at winches and capstans, swung bales from pier to deck.

Conan came striding down to the waterfront. In answer to his curt query, the captain of the harbor watch told him that Zarono's *Petrel* had departed more than an hour previously and had long since vanished behind the hook that formed the eastern horn of the harbor. Conan growled rude thanks, spun on his heel, and went clattering up the gangplank of his own vessel, the carack *Wastrel*.

'Zeltran!' he bellowed.

'Aye, Captain?' said the mate, who was ordering the placing of provisions in the hold. Zeltran was a short, rotund Zingaran with a long, sweeping black mustache. Despite his fat, he moved as lightly as a cat.

'Line the rascals up and call roll!' said Conan. 'We shove off as soon as we can!'

Presently the entire crew of buccaneers was assembled in the waist. The majority were swarthy Zingarans, with a sprinkling of other nationalities. Three were missing, and the ship's boy was sent scurrying to drag them out of the dives in which they had overslept their liberty. The rest of the crew, lashed on by Conan's voice, speeded up their leisurely loading of the ship.

The missing men at last appeared at a run; the last bale was stowed; the cables were cast off from the quay. Eight sailors strained at the oars of the longboat to tow the *Wastrel* out to open water. When the first hint of a sea breeze caused the sails to lift and flap, the longboat came alongside and was hauled aboard.

Then, as her sails filled, the *Wastrel* leaned with the wind; the ripple at her bow grew to a white curl of foam. She rocked gently and rhythmically as she met the swells of the open sea, and the squeal of the circling gulls mingled with the splash of the bow wave, the groan of timbers, the creak of cordage, and the sigh of the wind in the rigging.

Conan stood at the forward end of the quarterdeck, leaning on the rail and peering moodily past the edge of the mainsail at the distant horizon. Having given the course that Conan had commanded and organized the watches, Zeltran bustled up to stand beside the Cimmerian.

'Well, my Captain,' quoth he, 'and whither away this time?'

'Know you Black Zarono's *Petrel*?' said Conan.

'That big tub that put out an hour before you came to the ship? Aye, I know her. They say that Zarono's a skilled seaman but a hard, black-hearted man. He had connections among the lesser nobility; but they kicked him out, 'tis said, because of something he did that even those high-born reprobates wouldn't stand for. That's how he came to be a buccaneer. Be you at odds with Captain Zarono? Hes no copemate to take on lightly.'

'Keep it to yourself, rattlepate, and I'll tell you.' Conan gave Zeltran a brief account of Ninus, the chart, and Zarono. 'So,' he continued, 'if I catch him in open sea, I'll give him a proper taste of steel. If the *Petrel* is bigger, the *Wastrel* has finer lines and can beat closer to the wind.'

'Oh, aye, we can catch her,' said Zeltran, giving his mustache a fierce twirl. 'And I've no doubt that I could slay six or seven of Zarono's knaves all by myself. But, Captain, weren't it cleverer to follow him without letting him know, thus letting him lead you to the treasure?'

Conan turned a burning, slit-eyed gaze on the mate. Then he grinned and clapped the smaller man on the back.

'By Crom and Mannanan, little man,' he roared, 'you've earned your pay!' He glanced up to where a cluster of sailors, standing on the topsail footrope with one arm each about the yard, were awaiting the command to break out the topsail. 'Belay that!' he bellowed. 'Back to the deck, you!' He turned to Zeltran. 'We won't fly our topsail, because Zarono would see it, and we can sail as fast without ours as he can with his. Who is that man with the eagle sight?'

'Riego of Jerida?'

'That's the one. Put him in the top and let us see what he sees.'

The young Zingaran sailor was presently standing in the basket-shaped main top, peering toward the south-eastern horizon. He called down:

'Carack dead ahead, Captain. I see her topsail, and when a wave lifts her I can glimpse a black hull.'

'That's the *Petrel*,' said Conan. 'Steady as you go, helmsman. He turned to Zeltran, who stood tugging at his huge mustache. 'We'll hold back during the day, and at night draw close enough to glimpse his running light. With luck, he'll not even see us!'

Conan grinned hardily, with a gleam of pleasure in his eyes. He drew a deep breath, and expelled it in a gust. This was the life: a sound deck under heel, half a hundred hardy rogues at your command, a sea to sail and a foe to fight – and wild, red, roaring adventure in the offing!

With all sails but the telltale topsail spread, the *Wastrel* foamed southeastward on the track of the *Petrel*, as the blinding sun soared into the azure heavens and dolphins bounded out of the turquoise swells and plunged back in again.

Chapter 3

DEATH OF THE *SEA QUEEN*

THE CARAVEL *Sea Queen*, which served as the Zingaran royal yacht, had passed between the Zingaran coast and the Barachan Isles. This archipelago was a notorious nest of pirates – most of them Argosseans – but on this occasion none of their corsairs was scouring that part of the Western Ocean. Then the ship passed the boundary between Zingara and Argos.

The Argossean coast fell off to eastward. Following Chabela's commands, Captain Kapellez bore to port, but not so sharply as the coast curved. Hence the Argossean coast fell away until it was barely visible from the masthead.

There were two reasons for this course. One was to reach the coast of Shem near Asgalun as quickly as possible. The other was to lessen the chance that some mainland-based Argossean pirate or privateer might put out after them.

Now, however, a massive black carack had been visible aft since mid-morning. By early afternoon it had drawn close enough for the keenest-eyed sailor of the crew to make out its insignia.

' 'Tis naught to fear, my lady,' said Captain Kapellez. 'Yonder ship is but one of the privateers in the service of your royal sire. I make it out to be the *Petrel*, under Captain Zarono.'

Chabela was still not satisfied. There was something ominous about the steady approach of that bulky black hull. Of course, it might be happenstance that the other ship was following the same course as their own.

Neither was the name of Zarono reassuring. She hardly knew the man beyond a formal acquaintance at court functions, but sinister rumors wafted about concerning the buccaneer. One of her friends, the lady Estrellada, had passed on to Chabela the tale that Zarono was smitten with her, Chabela's, charms. But the princess had paid little heed to this, for unattached men around

39

the court were always smitten with the charms of a princess as a matter of course. There was always a chance that one or another would become a royal consort . . .

Now her suspicions were fully aroused. It was the third day after the *Sea Queen* had left Kordava, and by now her disappearance would have become general knowledge. In fact, the palace would be in an uproar.

The absence of the royal yacht from its usual mooring would have betrayed Chabela's method of flight. Since it was incredible that she would have headed north to the wild shores of Pictland, or west into the trackless wastes of the unexplored ocean, it was plain that she must have set her course southeast, along the coast of the main continent. There lay Argos, the city-states of Shem, and the sinister kingdom of Stygia 'ere one came to the black countries.

The disturbance over her disappearance might well, she thought, have been loud enough even to rouse King Ferdrugo from the lethargy that gripped him. He might have dispatched Zarono with a commission to hale his fugitive daughter back home.

Chabela murmured gracious but distracted words to the captain and turned away. After pacing the deck restlessly, she leaned her elbow on the rail, which was carved with leaping dolphins and trident-brandishing mermen. She watched the pursuing craft as if under a hypnotic spell.

The *Petrel* drew steadily nearer, its blunt bow smashing through the waves. At this rate, she thought, in another half-hour it would forge up to windward, blanketing the sails of the *Sea Queen* and bringing the smaller vessel to a halt.

Chabela was by no means ignorant of naval and nautical lore. Unlike her father, who detested the sea and never went near the *Sea Queen*, she had been a sailor girl ever since she was a small child. Only in the last few years, since she had grown into womanhood, had her father's strict commands stopped her practice of donning sailor garb and swarming into the rigging with the seamen.

The princess shivered, then forced herself to relax. The other carack had so far displayed no hostile or alarming intentions. A Zingaran privateer would hardly

40

be so insane as to attack the private yacht of the king of Zingara.

Then a shadow fell across the sun-bright deck. This shadow was, strangely, a dark green: an uncanny emerald shroud of mystic gloom.

Raising her head, the princess could see nothing to explain the weird nebulosity that now enshrouded the *Sea Queen*. No cloud lay athwart the sun; no flying monster hovered on flapping wings. Yet a shroud of emerald gloom had enveloped the *Sea Queen* like a dense though impalpable fog. The faces of the crew were pale and wide-eyed with fear.

Then terror struck. Tentacles of green gloom swirled about the nearest sailor, who shrieked with fear. Like the coiling limbs of some kraken of the deep, the shadowy tentacles enmeshed him. The girl caught one wild look at his white, despairing face and thrashing limbs. Then the green coils seemed to sink into his body and disappear. The burly seaman stiffened to statuesque immobility, while a green hue suffused his flesh and even his garments. He looked like a statue of jade.

Chabela cried out to Mitra. The entire ship was a mass of yelling, struggling men, battling with mad futility against the slithering coils of emerald mist that swept about them and sank into their flesh, transforming them into motionless green effigies.

Then ropy green tendrils curled about the princess herself. Her flesh crept with fear as she felt the touch of the impalpable stuff. At the touch, a chilling paralysis ran through her body. As the coils sank into her, a cold darkness closed down on her mind and she knew nothing more.

On the quarterdeck of Zarono's *Petrel*, the privateer watched with ill-concealed awe as the Stygian sorcerer worked his spell. Motionless as a dusty mummy, the Stygian squatted before an apparatus he had constructed as the carack approached the *Sea Queen*. This consisted of a small cone of dim, gray crystal, atop a low altar of black wood. The altar had the appearance of great age. It had once been elaborately carved, but the carvings were now largely worn away. Those that survived

41

showed minute naked human beings fleeing from a colossal serpent. The eyes of the serpent had originally been a pair of opals, but one had fallen out of its socket and been lost.

In response to Menkara's whispered incantation, the crystal cone had flashed into an eery radiance. A nimbus of pulsing emerald light had woven about it, illuminating the swart features of the mage and making his visage look more skull-like than ever.

When the nimbus of green light was actively pulsating, the Stygian had held before his face a mirror of black metal, framed by an iron wreath of intertwined monsters. As Zarono watched with mounting awe, the emerald radiance seemed to be drawn to the surface of the mirror and reflected thence to the distant deck of the *Sea Queen*. Faint in the sunlight, the green beam was nevertheless plainly visible, stretching straight across the heaving gap between the ships. Something was happening on the caravel, although Zarono could not quite see what because of the distance.

With the loss of control of her tiller, the *Sea Queen* lost seaway and lay wallowing with sails flapping. Zarono brought his carack alongside. The Stygian emerged from his trance and sagged wearily against the rail. His dark features were the color of dirty linen, and cold sweat bedewed his impassive countenance.

'I am done,' sighed Menkara. 'That conjuration taxes one's strength to the limit. And yet, it is no great spell, being easily warded off by one who knows how . . . But those silly beings yonder are ignorant of magical matters. Go; you will find them harmless to you for an hour.'

'Are they dead, then?'

'Nay; merely in a suspension of animation. Help me to my cabin.'

Zarono assisted the enfeebled sorcerer to his feet and led him, stumbling, to his quarters, while the boatswain carried the altar with its cone.

When he had closed the door upon the exhausted Stygian, Zarono wiped the sweat from his forehead with a lace kerchief. Wizardry was all very well, but it was a fearsome weapon. Far more would he, Black Zarono, prefer the clash of cutlasses, the whine of arrows and bolts, the smash of catapult balls, and the crash of a

bronzen ram into the side of a hostile ship. He had
committed not a few villainies in his career, but at least
they had been sins of the normal human kind, not this
dabbling with dark and perhaps uncontrollable powers
from unearthly planes and dimensions.

'Ernando!' he roared at the cook. 'A double flagon
of wine, and the strongest we have in the butts!'

Thus the *Sea Queen* was taken and, very shortly, died.
Boarders from the *Petrel* swung aboard, picked up the
frozen figure of the girl, and carried her to Zarono's
quarterdeck. Others piled combustibles around the bases
of the masts and doused the piles with oil. Then all
returned to the *Petrel* and shoved off with poles and
boathooks.

When there was a safe gap between the two ships, a
squad of archers lit fire arrows and discharged them at
the *Sea Queen*. In a few minutes, the piles caught fire.
One by one, the sails blazed up with a roar, spreading
black, charred fragments far and wide. Flames spread
over the ship, engulfing the living but motionless crew-
men.

The *Petrel* spread her sails again and plodded on-
ward toward the coast of Shem, leaving the blazing
wreck behind.

From the main top of his own carack, Conan gazed toward the mushroom of smoke that marked the end of
the *Sea Queen* and muttered an oath to his grim Cimmerian god, Crom. The *Wastrel* lay off the horizon to
the northwest, invisible from the deck of the *Petrel* —
although, had any of Zarono's folk thought to scan the
sea in that direction from the mastheads, they might
have glimpsed the tops of Conan's rigging as the *Wastrel*
rose on the swells.

From his eyrie, Conan had watched the doom of the
Zingaran royal yacht. Why Zarono should stop to destroy a ship of his own nation, Conan could not imagine. There must, he thought, be more to the plot than
a simple rape of a treasure chart and a dash to seize
the fabled hoard. But the mighty Cimmerian had long
ago learned to set aside unanswerable questions until

further information should cast light upon them, rather than futilely to brood and fret over them.

Whoever the unknown victims on the caravel were, he thought, he would avenge them at the same time that he settled his own score with Zarono. Perhaps he would soon have an opportunity.

Chapter 4

THE NAMELESS ISLE

SUNSET TRANSFORMED the cloudy vault of heaven into a canopy of burning splendor. Over the dark waves, flecked with crimson reflections, the blunt black bow of the *Petrel* threw up a snowy bow wave as she ran free to the southwest under a quartering west wind. Far behind her and unknown to any aboard her, Conan followed in the *Wastrel*, hovering just beyond easy detection under the burning sunset and later under the silently wheeling stars.

In the master's cabin, Zarono sprawled in his great chair, brooding over a silver goblet set with uncut smaragds. The bouquet of strong Shemitish wine filled the wood-paneled chamber. The swaying lamps, hung by chains from overhead, shed wavering light on crinkled parchments pinned to the walls between ribbed stanchions. The light winked on the jewels in the hilts of swords and daggers, which also adorned these walls.

Zarono's sallow features were gloomy and his cold black eyes withdrawn. He wore a loose, full-sleeved blouse of soiled white silk, with lacy ruffles at throat and wrist. His thick black hair was tousled, and he was deep in drink.

When knuckles rapped lightly on his door, he growled a curse, then called a grudging permission to enter. In came Menkara with the rolled chart in one hand. The lean Stygian surveyed the sprawled figure of the privateer with prim disfavor.

'More sorceries?' sneered Zarono, and hiccuped. 'Can you never leave an ordinary mortal to the pleasures of the vine, without thrusting your ugly face into his thoughts? Well, say your say.'

Without answering this flare of drunken temper, Menkara unrolled the chart on the table before Zarono and pointed a bony finger at the lines of cryptic glyphs wherewith the enigmatic scroll was inscribed.

'I have been puzzling over the Mitraist priest's chart

45

ever since we took it from him,' said the Stygian, with unusual tension in his normally dull and listless voice. 'The coastline shown here is obviously that of southerly Stygia. Although the language is unknown to me, I found that some of the captions bore a tantalizing familiarity. I have bent my intellect to the task of deciphering the inscription, while you have sat here swilling like a fool—'

Zarono flushed and started to rise, one hand going to the hilt of his sword. But Menkara halted him with a raised palm.

'Control your personal feelings, man. This is a matter of greater importance. Listen: I have studied comparable tongues in my magical apprenticeship, and I know that the ancient Valusian tongue, like those of ancient Stygia and Acheron, was writ with an alphabetic script, each symbol denoting a sound. Since certain parts of this chart show the lands we know as Shem and Stygia, with cities like Asgalun and Khemi, I was able to deduce the meaning of certain letters in the inscription, where they appear in the captions denoting these places. Other inscriptions seem to mark the sites of such vanished elder cities as Kamula and Python.'

The music of these devil-haunted names sent a chill of sobriety into Zarono's befuddled wits. Frowning, he bent forward to listen closely. Menkara continued:

'Thus, adding to my familiarity with this ancient tongue through the symbols representing known names, I was at length able to elucidate the inscription about this particular island, which I had never seen on a chart before.'

Zarono frowned at the dot on the chart indicated by Menkara's gaunt forefinger. 'Unknown to me as well, sorcerer. Pray continue.'

The Stygian went on: 'I deciphered the inscription marking this isle as something like *siojina-kisua*. Now, this would seem to be from the old Stygian word *siojina*, or at least a cognate thereto. And *siojina*, in the oldest known form of Stygian, may be rendered into Zingaran as "that which hath no name." '

Zarono's black, restless eyes, fully sober, were alight in his masklike ivory features. 'The Nameless Isle,' he whispered.

'Yes,' hissed Menkara with cold satisfaction in his reptilian gaze. 'That *kisua* means "island" we may be sure, for the same word occurs in connection with several other isles shown on this chart. He moved his forefinger from one dot to another, and another. 'And I assume that one of your piratical trade may have heard, ere now, the legends of this demon-haunted Nameless Isle: how it is a remnant of elder Valusia, wherein a mouldering ruin survives to attest the powers of the pre-human serpent-men.'

'I only know that sailors lore tells of an isle without a name, where lies the greatest treasure ever assembled in one place,' said Zarono.

'True,' said Menkara, 'but there is something else of which you may not know. There is loot enough of the usual kind, forsooth. But aside from tawdry gold and gems, it is said that here also lies a vast magical treasure – an authentic copy of the *Book of Skelos*.'

'I seek no accursed magic, but only honest gold!'

Menkara smiled thinly. 'Aye, but think. We fain would persuade the earth's mightiest magician to help our lord Villagro to the throne of Zingara. He would be pleased, of course, to see the cult of Set exalted and that of Mitra cast down. We could, however, truly win his favor and enlist his support by presenting him with so mighty a magical treasure as the *Book of Skelos*. It is a crime against the sacred science of magic that so potent a volume of ancient lore should languish neglected. It is thought that there are but three copies of the book in existence: one in a crypt beneath the royal library of Aquilonia, in Tarantia; one in a secret temple in Vendhya; and the third here.' The Stygian tapped the chart with his fingernail.

Zarono asked: 'Why, if this damned book is so precious, has none taken it yet from the Nameless Isle?'

'Because, until I saw this chart, neither I nor any other seeker after the higher truths knew precisely where the Nameless Isle lay. As you see, it lies afar from the coast of the black countries and from the isles we know. There is no land within a hundred leagues of it in any direction, nor lies it near the lanes of ships that ply between the ports of civilized lands. A mariner who sought it at random in that waste of waters could plow the sea forever without finding it – or at least until he was be-calmed without food and water and miserably perished.

'Futhermore, you know that sailors are a superstitious lot, whose fancies have peopled the southern sea with deadly reefs and man-eating monsters. It is no accident that the Nameless Isle has long been lost to knowledge.'

'Even with fair winds, 'twould take us several days to reach it from here,' mused Zarono, his long chin in his fist.

'What imports it? We have the girl safe, and a few days more or less will matter not. With the *Book of Skelos* as our bribe, the added certainty of enlisting Thoth-Amon will be well worth the delay. Nor, I think, are you insensible to the charms of gold.' The fires of fanaticism flickered in Menkara's normally expression-less eyes.

Zarono rubbed his jaw. While he cared nothing for magic, it seemed good to do everything possible to win the powerful prince of magicians to Duke Villagro's cause. And, could Zarono win the treasure of the Name-less Isle for his own, why, not only wealth but also rank, privilege, and respectability would again be his.

Decision flashed in his dark eyes. He sprang to his feet and pushed out the cabin door, bellowing: '*Vancho*!'

'Aye, Captain?' said the mate.

'Set course due south, until the pole star be but one point above the horizon!'

'Into the open sea, sir?' said Vancho incredulously.

'You heard me, damn your hide! Due south!'

Blocks rattled and ropes slapped as the *Petrel*'s yards rotated to take the wind right abeam on the starboard tack, and the carack's blunt bow swung into the new course across the star-spangled sea.

Menkara retired to his cabin to study the chart. He was afire with the lust for old and sinister knowledge. With the *Book of Skelos*, Thoth-Amon could become all-powerful. To help Villagro to a throne would be a mere trifle; the great Stygian wizard might even hold the empire of the world within his grasp. And, when the sons of Set held dominion over all lands, what might not be the fortune of the priest Menkara, who had made it all possible?

Conan thoughtfully followed the running light of the *Petrel* as the larger carack changed course from east-by-south to due south. He knew nothing of Chabela's presence aboard the *Petrel*, or Villagro's plot, or Menkara's ambitions. He only knew – or thought he knew – that Zarono had taken the chart from Ninus and was on his way to the Nameless Isle and its treasure. The reason for the sudden change of course he could not even guess.

The giant Cimmerian scrambled down the shrouds from the main top with the agility of a monkey. 'Zeltran!'

'Aye, Captain?'

'Six points to starboard! Full and by on the starboard tack! Follow the *Petrel*'s light!'

'Aye aye, sir. Start the starboard braces; helms down; trim the port braces . . . Helms up; straighten her out . . . Steady as you go . . .'

Conan stood silently at the quarterdeck rail as the *Wastrel* took her new course into strange waters. Once they left the coast of the continent, they would have no means of knowing where they were beyond the pole star, which, on clear nights, would tell them how far they had come in a north-south direction. Zarono had better know whither he was bound. If he got lost on the featureless plain of water, he would lose the *Wastrel* as well.

As far as Conan knew, the darkly glittering immensity of water before him ran clear to the world's edge. What might lie beyond it he could not even guess. Old legends whispered of fabulous islands, strange continents, unknown peoples, and weird monsters.

The legends might even be true. Less than a year had elapsed since, in this selfsame *Wastrel*, he had sailed with its former captain, the saturnine Zaporavo, to an unknown island in the West, where Zaporavo and several of the Zingaran crew had met their doom. Few things in Conan's adventurous life had been stranger or more sinister than the Pool of the Black One and its inhuman attendants. Now, for all he knew, he might be on his way to even deadlier perils.

He drew a deep breath and laughed gustily. Crom! A man can die but once, so what boots it to maunder over imaginary perils? Enough to combat the terror when you meet it, with steel in your hand and battle madness in your heart. He would take his chances with fate on the Nameless Isle, ahead of him on the rim of the world.

Chapter 5

AT THE WORLD'S EDGE

ALL NIGHT, the two caracks plied the warm southern waves. With dawn, the *Wastrel,* as she had done for the past five days, took in sail to drop back, so as not to be seen from the *Petrel* in the waxing light. With nightfall, if they had not yet reached the Nameless Isle, she would make up the time, since her slimmer hull and hollowed bow gave her an advantage in speed over the blunter, beamier *Petrel.*

Meanwhile the *Wastrel's* sharp stem cut through the endless hillocks of blue-green. Flying fish leaped from her forefoot to hurl themselves aloft, soar for half a bowshot, and plunge back into the sea. Neither carack had sighted another ship since taking the southerly course.

Presently a cluster of cloudlets appeared in an otherwise clear sky. The *Petrel* altered course to starboard, and in a few hours an island hove into view on the horizon, beneath the clouds.

From the *Petrel's* forecastle, Zarono thoughtfully scanned the unknown island. It looked innocuous enough: a tawny-sanded beach; tall, slender palms with emerald fronds. What lay beyond the fence of palm trunks, none could say as yet.

Menkara, a black cloak wrapped about his lean shoulders, joined Zarono. 'It is the island,' he said tonelessly.

Zarono's white teeth showed in his sallow face as he smiled. 'Aye, priest, so it is! Now about this treasure: how is it guarded? Ghosts, demons, or merely a few dragons? I count on your supernatural powers to shield us from harm while we loot the tombs or crypts or whatever they are. Vancho! Take her into yonder bay, if it prove deep enough . . .'

A quarter-hour later, Zarono commanded: 'Let go the anchor! Trice up all sails! Vancho, lower the first longboat and pick a landing party – all stout men, well armed.'

With much bustle and clatter, the boat was lowered and a dozen Zingarans, clanking with arms, swarmed down ropes to take their places on the thwarts. They pulled away from the *Petrel* to the beach. There they ran the boat's nose up on the sand, then piled out into shallow water to haul the boat farther up on the strand. Under the boatswain's command, they spread out along the beach, swords drawn and fingers on the triggers of crossbows, warily watching the palms. A small group pushed into the trees out of sight and presently re-appeared, waving an all-clear signal to the *Petrel*.

'Lower the other boat,' said Zarono. He and Menkara took their places, together with eight more sailors. Vancho remained aboard the *Petrel*.

The second boat reached the shore without incident. Zarono mustered his men. In a few minutes he, Menkara, and the bulk of the landing parties had vanished into the palms. Three buccaneers were left to guard the longboats: a swart, hook-nosed Shemite, a giant black from Kush, and a bald, red-faced Zingaran.

All of this Conan, in the main top of the *Wastrel*, observed with keen interest. His ship lay just over the horizon, hove to with her foresail backed and rolling uneasily in the long oceanic swells.

For a time, Zarono's party hacked its way through dense, tropical undergrowth. There was no sound save the grunts and heavy breathing of laboring men, the chopping sound of the blades of broadswords and cutlasses as they sheared through the stems of vines and saplings, and the rustle of leaves as the pirates pushed their way through the jungle.

The air was hot and steamy. Sweat glistened on muscular arms, matted bare chests, and scarred brows. The smell of decaying vegetation blended with that of exotic flowers, which blazed in gold and crimson and white against the dark green of the forest.

Zarono became aware of another odor, as well. It took him some time to recognize it. At last he realized, with a prickle of revulsion, that it was the musky stench of snakes. With a muttered curse, he pressed to his nostrils a gilded pomander ball, wherein scraps of citron peel and bits of cinnamon yielded a spicy scent. But even above the soothing smell of the pomander, he could still detect the odor of snakes. This puzzled him, when he thought about the matter. In his piratical career he had visited many small oceanic islands, and never had he known any to harbor serpents.

It was sweltering; the close-set palm trunks, draped with loops and curves of flowering lianas, cut off the fresh sea breeze. Soaked with sweat, Zarono probed the greenery about them with sharp black eyes. He spoke to Menkara:

'Save for this damnable stink of serpents, Stygian, I sense naught dangerous about your Nameless Isle.'

Menkara gave a wan, thin-lipped smile. 'Do you truly notice nothing, then?'

Zarono shrugged. 'Outside of the stench and the heat, no. I had expected supernatural terrors, and I am disappointed. No ghouls or specters – not even a gibbering, drooling thing from a tomb? Ha!'

Menkara gave him a coldly meditative stare. 'How dull are you Northerners' senses! Do you not even feel the silence?'

'Hm,' grunted Zarono. 'Now that you mention it. . .'

A cold prickling crawled over Zarono's flesh. Truly, the jungle was ominously silent. One would not expect large beasts on a small island; but still, there should have been the whir of birds, the rustle of scuttling lizards and land crabs, and the rattle of the fronds of the palms overhead as the breeze stirred them. But there was no sound at all, as if the jungle held its breath and watched them with unseen eyes.

Zarono muttered a curse but controlled his feelings. Busy hacking their way through the brush, the men had not yet noticed anything. Zarono signed Menkara to hold his tongue and plodded after his crew into the interior. But the sensation of being watched did not cease.

Toward midday, the buccaneers reached their goal. It was strange: pushing through a dense tangle, they suddenly found themselves in an open glade. The jungle ended abruptly, as if the foilage dared not cross an invisible boundary. Beyond that unseen circular barrier,

53

flat, sandy soil stretched away, bearing only a few withered-looking patches of lank, pale, colorless grass. Menkara and Zarono exchanged a meaningful glance.

Amidst this dead zone rose the mysterious edifice they had come to ravish. Zarono could not decide on the purpose of this structure; it might equally well be a tomb, a shrine, a temple, or a storehouse. It was a squat, heavy building of a dull, lusterless black stone, which seemed to soak up all the light that fell upon it, so that its physical outlines were difficult to discern.

The structure was of roughly cubical shape; but its surfaces, instead of being simple squares, were made up of a multitude of planes and curves of irregular form, oriented every which way. There was no symmetry to the structure. It was as if every part of the building had been designed by a different architect, or as if the building had been assembled from parts of a score of other structures chosen at random from many lands and eras.

The black temple – if such it was – loomed before them in the hazy light. Zarono felt the icy touch of an awe he had never before experienced. An aura of fear, radiating from the squat black thing, unmanned even that tough, steel-nerved ruffian. Blinking, he glared at it, striving to discover the source of the terror that made his breath come in quick gasps and caused his heart to pound.

The temple looked wrong. The style was like nothing he had seen in his far voyaging. Even the ghoul-haunted tombs of Stygia were not so alien as this irregular block of black stone. It was as if the builders had followed some inhuman geometry of their own – some unearthly canon of proportion and design.

Menkara's face was gray and pearled with sweat. He muttered, half to himself: 'It is as I thought. The Z'thoum Ritual has been enacted here.' He shivered. 'I had not thought that darksome rite had been uttered aloud these three thousand years . . .'

'What is it, yellow dog?' snarled Zarono, fear making him vicious.

The Stygian turned wide eyes upon him. 'A protective spell,' he whispered. 'One of very great power. Were any man fool enough to enter the precincts of the temple without the counter-spell, his presence would awaken that which sleeps therein.'

'Well? Have you this counter-spell?'

'Thanks be to a Father Set, I have. Little is known of the pre-human serpent-men of Valusia. But, from what little I know, I can weave the counter-spell, albeit I cannot maintain it for long.'

'Long enough to loot that black thing, I hope,' growled Zarono. 'Best that you set about it, man.'

'Then go back into the woods, you and your men, and face away from me,' said Menkara.

Zarono herded his buccaneers back into the brush, where they formed a cluster, with their backs to the clearing. They listened with tight lips as Menkara's voice rolled on in an unknown tongue. What else he did, they did not know. But the light diffused through the foilage seemed to flicker, as of shadows passing and repassing overhead. The Stygian's voice seemed to be echoed from above by other, inhuman voices that spoke with a dry, rasping tone, as if their vocal organs were never designed for human speech. The earth trembled slightly, and the light dimmed as if a cloud had passed athwart the sun . . .

At last Menkara, in a weak voice, called: 'Come!'

Zarono found the Stygian looking aged and bent. 'Hasten,' Menkara murmured. 'The counter-spell will not hold for long.'

Pale and sweating, Zarono and Menkara entered the temple. Within, there was little light save that which entered through the open portal, and the dull black stone absorbed this light with little reflection.

At the far end of the irregular chamber rose a huge black altar, and on top of this altar squatted an idol of gray stone. The idol was that of a being that combined the qualities of a man and a toad, with its male characteristics obscenely exaggerated. Toadlike, with a bloated, warty skin, it squatted on the altar. The surface of the gray stone had a rough, crumbly appearance, as if the stone itself were rotting and sloughing away.

The idol's toothless mouth was slightly open in a mirthless grin. Above the mouth, a pair of pits corresponded to nostrils, and above these a row of seven globular gems, set in a row, corresponded to eyes. The seven gems faintly reflected the light that came through the portal.

Shuddering at the aura of cosmic evil that radiated from the thing, Zarono tore his eyes away from it. Before the altar lay two small sacks of old leather. One had burst at the seam, and a glittering trickle of gems had poured from it to make a puddle of granulated splendor on the stone pave, shining in the dimness like a constellation sighted through a gap in the clouds.

Beneath the sacks of jewels was a huge book, bound in the hide of some reptile and fitted with clasps and hinges of bronze, green with age. The scales of the reptile whose skin formed the cover were of a size that no earthly beast had worn for eons.

The two men exchanged one wordless, triumphant glance. Zarono gathered up the burst sack, carefully so as not to spill out any more of the gems. When he had cradled it in the crook of one arm, he picked up the other sack with his free hand. Then Menkara pounced upon the book, raised it, and clasped it to his bosom. His gaunt visage was flushed and his eyes humid with a strange, darkling ecstasy. Without a word or a backward glance, they tiptoed out of the temple, crossed the clearing almost at a run, and rejoined the buccaneers who awaited them uneasily at the edge of the jungle.

'Back to the ship, and yare!' said Zarono.

All hastened back along the trail they had cut, eager to leave behind this seat of ancient evil, over which accursed forces still hovered, and regain the clear air and blessed sunlight of the open sea.

Chapter 6

FLAMING EYES

THE PRINCESS Chabela had passed through terror and
fury into relative calm. She knew not why the traitor
Zarono had turned against his liege lord to destroy his
royal vessel, nor why the buccaneer had captured her.
But she was no longer paralyzed by fear, for at least
her hands were free.

Zarono had locked her in a small cabin with her
hands tied behind her back with a length of silken
scarf. The flimsy length of scarlet silk seemed unsuited
for bonds; but Zarono had learned from a wandering
Vendhyan mountebank the art of knotting a cord so
as to defy the deftest fingers, and the scarlet fabric, for
all its lightness, seemed as tough as rawhide. At meal
times, Zarono himself came to the cabin to untie her
and later bind her up again. He refused to answer her
questions.

Chabela, however, bore beneath her girdle a small
knife. It was common for highborn Zingaran women to
carry such a blade, wherewith to end their lives when
menaced by brutal rape.

The resourceful girl put the knife to another use. By
stretching and straining, she got her hands on the bulge
where lay the knife and teased it out from its concealment. Then she wedged the hilt into a cavity in the
wooden scrollwork that formed a sill for the porthole.
She withdrew the sheath from the blade and, with her
back to the knife, she forced her wrists against the naked
blade.

The task was hard, for she could not see behind her
at such close quarters, and from time to time the bitter
kiss of the razor-sharp steel burnt her shrinking flesh.
Before she had sawn the silk through, her wrists were
slick with blood. But at last it parted.

Chabela took the knife from its place, returned it to
its sheath, and hid it again in her girdle. The silk, now

in two pieces, she used to bandage the several small, superficial cuts she had inflicted upon herself.

Now that she was free, how should she use her freedom? Zarono had left the ship, for she had overheard his last commands. Only part of the crew was left aboard, but Chabela knew that a burly seaman was posted outside the door to her cabin, which in any case was bolted from the outside.

That left the porthole, which looked upon a turquoise sea, a stretch of cream-colored beach, and a fringe of palms, thrusting emerald fronds against the clear blue of the sky.

Luckily for her, Chabela was far stronger, bolder, and braver than most of the delicate noble damsels of the Zingaran court. Few of them would even have dared to attempt what she next did. She opened the casement of the porthole and pulled her gown up through her girdle until the hem was above her knees. Below, a lazy swell rose and fell, a couple of fathoms below the porthole.

Quietly, Chabela wormed her way through the opening, lowered herself until she hung by her hands, and let go. She struck the water feet-first with a small splash, disappeared beneath the surface, and quickly bobbed up again, spitting water and brushing her heavy black hair back from her face. The water, though not cold, was cooler than the hot, humid air, and its coolness sent a shock through the princess's nerves. The brine stung her cuts.

Chabela had no time to enjoy the cool embrace of the sea. At any moment a seaman, idly leaning on the rail, might espy her and sound the alarm. Above her rose the ship's high stern, checkered with the panes of the after portholes. Above them, the rail of the poop deck and the masts and rigging swayed gently against the sky.

There would be a seaman posted on the poop somewhere, but at the moment no man's head showed above the rail. If she kept astern of the ship, she would be less likely to be seen than if she came abeam of it, where she would be exposed to the glances of men in the waist and the bow.

It was a long swim. To be inconspicuous, Chabela

swam on her back. Allowing only her face to emerge from the water, she swam parallel to the beach, to keep the ship's stern castle between herself and the rest of the vessel. When she tired, she floated for a while, sculling languidly with her hands.

At last the bulk of the *Petrel* shrank until the figures of men could no longer clearly be seen, even when they were visible. Then Chabela turned shoreward and struck out vigorously.

At last, trembling with fatigue, she felt the sandy bottom beneath her and dragged herself out on the yellow-gray beach. A few steps took her into the shade of the palms, where she crouched among a thick growth of ferns to rest.

She had, she thought, plunged from one peril to the other, for none knew what terrors the island might harbor. If nothing else befell her, she might run into Zarono and his rascals. But, putting her faith in Mitra, she still thought that she was better off than if she had remained in the hands of her enemies on the ship.

When she recovered her strength, she rose and moved about, casting around for a direction to take. She winced as pebbles and twigs dented the soles of her bare feet; for she had not, in recent years, had many chances to go barefoot. The breeze, sighing through the palms, chilled her damp garment and made her sneeze. Impatiently, she doffed her girdle and pulled the gown off over her head. The afternoon sun, slanting through the palm trunks along the beach, threw bars of sunlight on the healthy, olive-hued skin that covered her well-rounded form.

She wrung the remaining water out of the gown and spread it on the ferns to dry. With her knife she cut a strip from the hem, divided it in two, and wrapped a piece around each foot.

When the gown had dried, she resumed it, letting it hang only to knee length. Having recovered her strength, she set out to explore, holding the small knife in one capable fist. It was no sword, but it was better than nothing.

As she penetrated inland, the sweltering jungle closed about her. The sweetish smell of rotting vegetation and tropical blooms assailed her nostrils. Rough trunks, the saw-edged stems of palm fronds, and thorny lianas snagged her gown and tore it. They raised long red scratches on her arms and legs.

Further inland, the underbrush thinned somewhat, but the uncanny silence made her uneasy. Here the wind seemed not to penetrate. Her heart thudded.

She tripped on a root and fell. She struggled up, but then she tripped again. The third time, she realized that she was nearing the limits of her endurance. She had to force her aching limbs to carry her on.

Suddenly, a massive figure loomed up directly in her path, a dark form with burning eyes. She screamed, tried to leap back, and fell again. The figure lunged for her.

Conan thoughtfully scanned the sea. There lay Zarono's *Petrel,* anchored in the bay. To Zeltran he said:

'We could sweep in upon her and take her, with only part of her crew aboard. Then Zarono would find his retreat cut off when he returned. What say you, eh?' The Cimmerian gave his mate a fierce grin, as if he were already leaping aboard the other deck and mowing down the crew of the *Petrel* with his huge cutlass.

Zeltran shook his head. 'Nay, Captain, I like it not.'

'Why not?' snorted Conan. A headlong attack suited his barbarian nature, but he had still learned caution in his years of adventuring ashore and at sea. He knew that the stout little Zingaran, while brave enough in battle, was also shrewd and practical – a man of cunning counsels, which it was well to heed.

Zeltran turned crafty little black eyes upon Conan. 'Because, my Captain, we know not how many men Zarono left aboard. His crew is larger than ours, and those on the ship might still outnumber us.'

'Crom, I could take on half those knaves singlehanded!' The mate scratched the black stubble on his chin.

'No doubt, Captain, you are worth a dozen of the foe. But the rest of our crew would not fight with equal ferocity.'

'Why not?'

'Zaronos crew are fellow Zingarans and buccaneers. Our men would not wish to shed their brothers' blood without a stronger cause than we can show them. Besides, the *Petrel* is a larger ship with higher sides than ours, and therefore easy to defend against us. And did you mark the catapult on the forecastle?

'Nay, my Captain, if I understood you at the start of this cruise, we are here for treasure, not for the mere pleasure of a fight – the outcome of which would be doubtful in any case. Now, to get the treasure, meseems the most practical way were to sail around to the other side of the isle. Then our shore party can strive to reach the treasure ahead of Zarono's rogues. If we fail to do so, then we can count the number that Zarono brought ashore and weigh our chances of falling upon them and snatching the loot from them . . .'

After further argument, Conan gave in, although it went against his grain. 'Take her around the north end of the island,' he ordered glumly. 'Brace yards; carry on. Full and by on the starboard tack.'

He was, after all, no longer a lone berserker, free to throw his life away on a whim. As a leader of men, he had to consider their welfare, their wishes, and their whims as well as his own. But he still longed at times for the freedom of the wild, reckless years behind him.

A few hours later, the *Wastrel* dropped anchor on the eastern side of the island, where a headland provided some shelter against a sudden blow from the north. Conan filled his two ship's boats with armed men and rowed ashore across the sparkling waters. They beached and hauled the boats up the yellow-gray sands out of the reach of the tide.

Slapping his cutlass against his booted leg, the giant Cimmerian glowered around him at the tawny wet sand and the silent green wall of vegetation. The island seemed strangely gloomy, enshadowed, while all the sea around it was drenched in fierce tropical sunlight.

The boats secured and two burly buccaneers left on guard, Conan and the main body of his men plunged into the wall of fronds and ferns and vanished from view.

At length, Conan and his landing party reached the circular clearing in the jungle. The zone of dead grass and bare earth lay empty under the dull light. From the edge of the woods, Conan, frowning, swept the empty glade with his eyes. He saw no sign of life, but either the jungle or the squat black temple might hide a lurking foeman.

As for the temple, Conan did not at all like its looks. Its aura of brooding menace sounded a warning within him. The hairs of his nape prickled, and his heavy black brows shaded his eyes of volcanic blue. That the black enigma was the work of other than human hands, he did not doubt.

Perhaps, he thought, it was the work of the fabled serpent-men of Valusia. The dizzy geometry, the unintelligible and half-effaced sculptured decorations, and the zone of bare earth and dead or straggling grass all reminded him of a similar structure that he had seen years before in the grasslands of Kush. That, too, had been the handiwork of a long-gone pre-human race.

Instinct told him to turn from this dismal place and avoid that lowering structure. But within the edifice, Conan was sure, lay that for which he had come. To his men, Conan muttered:

'Stay hidden, keep quiet, and watch for any danger!'

Loosening his cutlass in its scabbard, he issued from the jungle and swiftly strode across the barren earth to the yawning maw of the mysterious citadel. In an instant, he had vanished from the sight of his comrades.

Ignoring the sepulchral chill that struck him as he strode through the portal, Conan slunk warily within, drawing his cutlass as he came. The broad blade gleamed in the dull light. His lambent gaze flickered over the stone toad-idol that squatted atop the altar and came to rest on the pavement in front of the plinth. Then he stopped short.

Whatever treasure had lain there was gone. Nor had it been long gone. The floor was thick with dust, and in this dust were writ two sets of footprints, coming and going. One set was of sea boots; the other, of sandals.

Zarono and one other, thought Conan.

In front of the altar, an oblong space was free of dust, save where scuffing feet had brushed it into that bare, dustless rectangle. In this clean oblong lay several gems, winking from the places where they had fallen from the burst bag. Zarono in his haste had neglected to gather them up.

Snarling a curse, Conan stepped forward, meaning to sweep up this remaining handful of jewels. It infuriated him to play the part of jackal to Zarono's lion; but neither would he, if he could help it, come away completely empty-handed.

Then he checked again. The stone idol had begun to move. The seven eyes, in a row above the wide, lipless mouth, were no longer mere dim, dusty globes of crystal, but living orbs wherein green flame blazed down upon the Cimmerian with cold, merciless fury.

Chapter 7

THE TOAD-THING

'CROM! It lives!' A grunt of astonishment was torn from Conan.

He tensed as a thrill of supernatural premonition set his pulse to pounding. And indeed, the scabrous stone idol was now imbued with a ghastly semblance of life. Swollen limbs moved and stretched.

Fixing its flaming eyes upon its prey, the idol hunched forward on its pedestal and toppled over the edge, to land with a crash on the stone floor where lay the winking gems. Its four-fingered forelimbs broke its fall, and without pause it advanced at an ungainly but surprisingly swift scuttle upon Conan. Its stony limbs rasped and grated against the stone of the floor. It was as bulky as a buffalo, and its seven green-glowing eyes were on a level with his own.

Conan started to swing his cutlass but wiser counsel prevailed in his mind. From the sound the creature made in moving, it was still composed of stone, even if living stone. Steel could do naught against it; a blow would merely shatter his blade and deliver him into its gaping maw.

Before the lipless mouth could engulf him, Conan whirled and bolted out into the clearing. No need for caution now; he roared:

'Back to the ship! And yare!'

Cries of astonishment and fear burst from the men, huddled at the edge of the clearing, as the toad-thing issued from the temple, close on Conan's heels. No second command was needed. With a swish of palm fronds and a crackle of shrubs, the buccaneer shore party took to its heels. And after them came the monster of living stone, ambling as fast as a man could run. Conan paused long enough to be sure that its attention was fixed upon himself and then set off in a different direction, to draw it after him.

'What's this? A wench, here? By the breasts of Ishtar and the belly of Dagon, this cursed isle has more surprises than ever I dreamed!'

The voice – human, albeit rough and speaking Argossean with an uncouth accent – roused Chabela and at the same time reassured her. Catching her breath, she accepted the hand that the tall figure, which had appeared so suddenly before her, thrust out to help her to rise. The man continued to speak:

'Here, lass, did I be startling you? Fry my guts, I meant no harm. How came ye to this gods-forsaken place at the world's edge?'

Her first panic allayed, Chabela saw that the man who had startled her was a burly, blond young giant in tattered seaman's garb. He was not one of Zarono's ruffians, but an honest-looking fellow with a fair skin reddened by sunburn, frank blue eyes, and unshorn locks and beard of fiery red-gold. A northman from his coloring, she thought.

'Zarono,' she panted, breasts still heaving from exhaustion and startlement. She swayed and might have fallen had not the red-haired seaman seized her arm in a calloused grip to steady her.

'That black swine, eh? Stealing young girls is he, now? Well, broil me for a lubber, I'd as soon spit the dog as look at him; but by Heimdal's horn and Mitra's sword, you're safe now. My crew will give you sanctuary, fear not – but what's toward?'

The northerner turned, one red-knuckled hand grasping the hilt of the huge cutlass that swung from his girdle as a crashing and thrashing in the brush sounded nearer and nearer. Then a tall figure burst from the cover of the foilage and paused at the sight of them. To her astonishment, Chabela knew the man.

'Captain Conan!' she cried.

Conan's eyes narrowed, taking in the blond stalwart with the half-drawn cutlass and the black-haired girl behind him, whose tattered gown scarcely hid her voluptuous form. The girl looked vaguely familiar to him, but he had no time to explore the matter.

'Run, you two!' he bellowed. 'The temple monster's after me! Come along; we'll talk later!'

A heavier crashing in the woods, from the direction

whence Conan had come, lent force to his commands. 'Look alive!' he yelled, snatching Chabela's wrist into his great paw and dragging her after him helter-skelter along the trail. The northerner ran after them. For a moment they seemed to have outdistanced their pursuer. When they stopped to pant, Conan said to the northman:

'Is there no hill or cliff on this accursed isle? The stone toad-thing could not climb.'

'By Woden's league-long spear, mate, nary a hill,' said the other, red-faced and gasping. 'Naught higher than this, save for a spit at the northeast, where the land rises to a cliff o'erhanging the main. But that's no good; the land rises slow like, and the idol could climb . . . Here it comes again!'

'Show us the way to this headland,' said Conan. 'I have a plan.'

The northerner shrugged and led them off through the jungle. When Chabela faltered, Conan scooped her up into his arms. The buxom girl was no lightweight, but the giant Cimmerian carried her without visible effort. Behind them, the crashing of the monster through the woods came clearly.

An hour later, as the sun sank towards the blue horizon, the three of them, scratched, tattered, and bone weary, reached the rise of land. The spit was triangular, tapering to an angle as it rose, like the bow of a ship. Conan remembered seeing this feature from the *Wastrel* as his ship rounded the north end of the island on its way to its present anchorage.

The northman had relieved his Cimmerian comrade of the girl's weight. Side by side the pair staggered out of the jungle and up the slope. Halfway to the apex of the point, the northman set Chabela down, and the two adventurers paused to see if the stone devil still pursued them.

It did, as a waxing noise of crashing and a motion of the vegetation testified.

'Well, Crom and Mitra, what's your plan?' gasped the red-haired man.

'Up to the point,' growled Conan, leading the way thither. At the very top, he leaned over the edge and looked down. A hundred feet below, the sea foamed back and forth over a broad reef of tumbled black rocks, whose sharp angles thrust up through the surf and whose surfaces gleamed wetly as the swells came and went among them. Amid the fangs of the reef lay a few tidal pools, some as much as a fathom square.

Chabela, looking back, gave a little shriek as the hulking shape appeared at the edge of the jungle. With a snapping of ferns and brush, it lumbered out into the open. Its seven eyes sighted the three fugitives at once, and it began advancing rapidly up the slope, with a gait like that of a man crawling as fast as he could on hands and knees.

'It has us cornered,' said the northman. 'Is't abandon ship for poor sailors at last?'

'Not yet,' said Conan. In a few terse phrases he explained his plan.

Meanwhile, the toad-thing continued its advance, its seven eyes blazing in the light of the setting sun. As it neared its prey, it changed its gait from a rapid crawl to a series of toad-like leaps. The ground shook beneath it as its vast stone weight came down at the end of each hop. Closer and closer it came, its lipless mouth opening in anticipation.

Conan stooped and picked up several loose stones. 'Now!' he shouted.

At his word, Chabela ran along the edge of the cliff, away from him. The red-haired man ran along the brink in the opposite direction, leaving Conan, on the very lip of the cliff, to face the monster alone.

As the two fugitives raced away in opposite directions, the toad-thing paused between hops, its green eyes swiveling, as if pondering which course to take.

'Come on!' roared Conan, hurling a stone. The missile struck with a sharp crack and bounced off the toad-thing's nose. A second followed, striking one of the eyes with a clank. The stone flew high, but the green flame in the eye faded, as if the stone had cracked the substance of which the orb was composed.

Before Conan had time to cast a third stone, the thing was upon him. It gathered its massive hind-limbs for a final hop that would bring it down right at the point of the cliff. Its wide mouth gaped in anticipation.

As the toad-thing left the ground, and while it was still in the air, Conan turned and leaped from the cliff. He flipped over in mid-air and, straight as an arrow, dove headfirst into the largest of the tidal pools below. He struck the water with his outstretched hands, angled to bring him instantly back to the surface.

Up on the cliff, the monster came down from its final leap on the very spot where Conan had stood. Its forefeet struck the edge, which crumbled under the impact with a shower of loosened stones and dirt. The forefeet slipped over the edge, and the momentum of the monster sent its body sliding after. For a second it hung poised on the crumbling lip of the cliff. Then it overbalanced and, with a roar of shattered stone, slid all the way over. It seemed to hang for an instant in mid-air, turning slowly over and over. Then it came down with an ever-speeding rush, to strike the rocks at the foot of the cliff with a mighty crash.

Dripping, Conan pulled himself out of the tidal pool and raked the hair out of his eyes. He had not quite landed in the center of the pool; hence a tear in his garments exposed a blood-oozing weal along ribs and thigh, where he had grazed one of the sharp rocks that lined the pool. He ignored the hurt to examine the remains of the toad-thing.

Stone might be magically imbued with life, but it was still stone. The monster had shattered into a hundred pieces, which lay hither and yon among the rocks at the base of the cliff. It took close scrutiny to discern that one of the stones composing that part of the reef had been one of the creature's feet, and that another had composed a part of its head. The other fragments blended into the rocky confusion as if they had lain there for eons.

Scrambling and hopping from rock to rock, Conan picked his way along the foot of the cliff until the bluff became low enough for him to scramble up. Then he turned back and rejoined his two companions on the spit. The red-haired man was leaning over the edge and contemplating the remains of the toad-thing below.

'Now by the claws of Nergal and the guts of Marduk, mate, that be a goodly sight to look on! But, now that we've outfaced that peril together, 'tis time we were beknownst to one another. I be Sigurd of Vanaheim, an honest seaman marooned on this cursed shore with his crew by shipwreck. And you?'

Conan was staring at Chabela. 'By Crom!' he said at last. 'Aren't you Chabela? Ferdrugo's daughter?'

'Aye,' said the girl, 'and you are Captain Conan.'

She had spoken his name before, when he had come upon her while fleeing from the toad-thing; and this recognition had provided the clue to her identity. Buccaneer captain and royal princess did not mingle familiarly at the royal court of Zingara. Nonetheless, Conan had seen her often enough at feasts, parades, and other ceremonials.

Since the greater part of their loot went to the crown, it behoved King Ferdrugo to play host to his buccaneer captains on occasion. The long legs, massive Shoulders, and grimly impassive features of the giant Cimmerian had made their mark in Chabela's mind, while he had recognized her readily enough despite her tattered garment, her disheveled hair, and the lack of cosmetics on her boldly handsome features.

'What in the name of all the gods are you doing here, Princess?' he demanded.

'Princess!' cried Sigurd, appalled. His ruddy face redder than ever, he stared at the half-naked girl whom he had handled so roughly and addressed with such familiarity. 'Ymir's beard and Baal's blazing fires, Highness, ye must forgive my tongue. A highborn lady, and I called her "lass" . . .' He sank to one knee, casting a stricken glance at Conan, who stood grinning.

Chabela said: 'Rise, Master Sigurd, and think no more of the matter. Royal etiquette were as out of place here as a horse on a housetop. Know you Captain Conan, my other rescuer?'

'Conan . . . Conan,' mused Sigurd. 'The Cimmerian?'

'Aye,' grunted Conan. 'You've heard of me?'

'Aye, I've heard tales in Tor—' Sigurd checked himself.

'In Tortage, you were about to say?' said Conan. 'I thought you had a look of the Barachas about you. I was one of the Brotherhood, too, until they made things too hot for me there. Now I'm captain of the *Wastrel*, a privateer for the Zingaran court. Is it friends?'

'Aye, by Lir's fish-tail and Thor's hammer!' said the Vanr, gripping Conan's hand in his. 'But we must take care not to let our lads get to fighting. Mine be mostly Zingarans; and the twain will be at each other's throats in the wink of an eye. Since neither of us belong to them two breeds, there's no reason for us to let that old feud disturb us.'

'Right,' said Conan. 'How came you and your men here?'

'We ran aground on a rock off the southern point and broke up. We made it to shore and saved most of our gear and victuals, but our captain took sick and died. I was mate, so I've been leader for the past moon, whilst we've worked at trying to make a sailing raft seaworthy enough to carry us to the mainland.'

'Know you aught of the black temple?'

'Oh, aye; my lads and I took a peek in that black shrine, but it fair reeked of evil and we shunned it thereafter.' Sigurd's blue eyes peered out to westward, where the red ball of the sun was just touching the blue horizon. 'Fry me for a lubber, lad, but all this jungle-chasing and monster-wrestling has given me a powerful thirst. Let's on to my camp and see if maybe we can rustle a drop of wine for the good of our souls! There's little enough left, but what there is we've earned today, I'm thinking.'

Chapter 8

THE COBRA CROWN

ZARONO RAVED and fumed when he returned to the *Petrel* and learned that Chabela was missing. The sailors who had been standing watch on the poop deck and outside Chabela's cabin were keelhauled at his command.

Before dawn the next day, he brought all but a few of his men ashore again. The day was spent in combing the island for the missing princess, who was an essential element in his plans. A few wisps of fabric torn from her gown were discovered; but these, while they testified to her having been there, shed no light on her present whereabouts.

The men also discovered the remains of Sigurd's camp. Of the Barachan pirates themselves, however, there was no trace.

At sunset a baffled Zarono, more furious than ever, returned to the *Petrel*. 'Menkara!' he shouted.

'Aye, Captain Zarono?'

'If your witcheries be good for aught, now's the time for them. Show me whither this damnable chit has fled!'

Soon afterwards, Zarono sat in his cabin and watched the Stygian set up his apparatus for the spell he had worked in Duke Villagro's dungeon. The brazier hissed; the sorcerer chanted:

'*Iao, Setesh . . .*'

The jade-green cloud of smoke condensed, and in the cloud a seascape took form. It showed a calm sea, in the midst of which lay a lean, graceful carack with all sails set. But the sails hung limply from the yards, while the ship rocked gently on smooth, oily swells.

'Conan's *Wastrel*, becalmed,' said Zarono when the vision had dissolved. 'But where?'

Menkara spread his hands. 'I'm sorry, but my art does not tell me. If the sun were still visible, I could at least tell you in what direction they are headed. As it is . . .'

'You mean,' snarled Zarono, 'that they could be anywhere over the horizon, but you have no way of telling whither?'

'I am not the great Thoth-Amon. What I can, I do.'

'Could you see if the girl was aboard?'

'Nay, but I am sure she was, or the vision would not have shown the ship. Doubtless she sleeps in one of the cabins.'

'I should have taken my pleasure of the drab whilst I had the chance,' growled Zarono. 'But what's to do now?'

'Well, the *Wastrel* might be bound for the coast of Kush; but more likely she is headed back for Kordava. Your Captain Conan would hasten to return the princess to Kordava in hope of a rich reward from the king.'

'If we crack on sail to northward, could we overtake them?'

'I think not. The ocean is too wide, and a calm that halts Conan's ship would also halt yours. They might sail northeast, to make landfall on the coast of Shem and seek aid of the king's brother Tovarro. We have no way of knowing. But you forget our main purpose.'

'The wench and the treasure were the main purpose!'

'Nay, I speak of the great Thoth-Amon. Once we enlist his aid, it matters not whether the princess be returned to her father, or whether she fetches home her uncle. The prince of sorcerers can control the lot as easily as a puppet-master jerks the strings of his marionettes. Let us sail northeastward to the Stygian coast. If on the way we overhaul Conan's ship, well and good; if not, it will not matter.'

From the Stygian coast, Zarono and Menkara took passage overland by caravan. Half the crew were left behind to guard the *Petrel*, while the other half, armed to the teeth, came with their captain. The passage cost Zarono good gold, which much grieved the Zingaran's larcenous heart.

Like most seamen, Zarono was uncomfortable on land. He felt out of his element and vaguely helpless. While a desert may be the closest earthly analogue to

the sea, it was still foreign to him. He liked neither the
rhythmically lurching gait of the ill-tempered camel nor
the dry desert air, which sucked every drop of moisture
from his gullet.

These discomforts, however, he must needs endure.
And by the third day, the Oasis of Khajar became
visible on the horizon. It was a dark and lonely clump
of motionless palms, ringed about a strange black pool.
Amidst the foliage, the outline of a massive edifice could
be espied.

They approached the oasis with caution. Menkara
rode in front, so that his garments, denoting him as a
priest of Set, should be visible to any watching eye.

Quiet hung over the oasis. No birds paddled about the
pool or fluttered and squawked in the palms. No sentinel
challenged them. At the edge of the oasis they halted.
On command, the camels lay down, a joint at a time,
perilously tilting their passengers. Zarono told the
boatswain:

'Keep your eye on the camel driver. The dogs are
frightened, and they might try to flee and leave us
stranded.'

Then Zarono and Menkara set out afoot, around the
edge of the sullen black pool, toward the massive
building in the background. Zarono did not like the look
of the pool. Black as liquid coal, it glistened in the
bright afternoon light. Oily colors coiled on its motionless surface, slowly writhing with a semblance of life.
To one side stood a block of reddish stone, resembling
an altar. Dark, rusty stains besmeared the top and sides
of the altar. Zarono, whose vices were merely the normal
ones, paled and shuddered at the thought of what might
arise betimes from the black mirror of the pool to con-
sume the victims of the altar.

They skirted the sinister pool and approached Thoth-
Amon's abode. As the palms opened out before them,
they saw that this edifice was, like the altar, made of
massive blocks of red sandstone. It was a large structure,
better called a palace than a mere house. The surface
and edges of the stone were worn, testifying to great age.

What lost age had reared this huge pile, none could
say. The glyphs carved in the arch over the doorway
were unlike any that Zarono had seen in his wide travels.

The design of the building was severely plain. Zarono found it hard to relate it to any known architectural style, save perhaps the massive pyramids that rose from the desert near Khemi. The effect was less that of a dwelling than that of a tomb.

The black doorway gaped like a yawning mouth in the hulking, brutal mass of sandstone. Menkara strode without pause up to those stone jaws and traced a cryptic sign in the air. Zarono, with a twinge of awe, saw that the sign glowed lines of green fire in the air for some moments after that bony finger had traced it.

Within, all was dark stone and echoing silence. There was no sign of any guards or servants. Menkara strode confidently forward, and Zarono could only follow.

Beyond the antechamber, a flight of stone steps, worn into smooth curves by many ages of sandaled feet, led down into darkness. Down below the level of the desert they descended, until they came at last to a level space. Advancing, they emerged into a hall.

Here was light – a sinister green glow from serpentine torcheres of polished copper. By the flickering emerald luminescence, Zarono could see that the hall was lined with two rows of huge, monolithic columns, graven with cryptic glyphs of the same kind that he had seen over the outer doorway. At the end of the column-lined hall, a man sat on a throne of black, glittering stone. As the two travelers approached, the man became clear to Zarono's sight.

The man was a dusky giant, with broad shoulders and aloof, hawklike features. From his shaven skull to his sandaled feet, his skin was a deep, rich brown. Black eyes glittered hypnotically from the depths of cavernous eye-sockets. He wore a simple white linen robe. The only ornament to be seen on his person was a copper-colored ring, in the form of a serpent that, making three turns around one finger of a muscular hand, held its tail in its jaws.

In a flash of insight, Zarono, from the severe plainness of the building and from the lack of adornment of the mighty sorcerer, divined something of the inner nature of Thoth-Amon. Here was a man to whom material possessions and showy gauds meant nothing. His passion was for something intangible – for power over his fellow men.

As they halted a few paces from the throne, the man spoke in a strong, clear voice: 'Greetings, Menkara, little brother!'

Menkara sank to all fours and touched his forehead to the black flagstones. 'In the name of Father Set, dread lord,' he whispered, 'I am come.'

The disquieting thought came to Zarono that even the priest was frightened. Zarono found himself sweating despite the dryness of the desert air.

'Who is this black-visaged Zingaran whom you have brought to my place?' queried Thoth-Amon.

'Captain Zarono, a buccaneer, dread lord: an emissary from Villagro, duke of Kordava.'

The cold, serpentine eyes leisurely looked Zarono up and down. Zarono had the feeling that the intelligence behind that ophidian gaze was so far removed from earthly considerations that the doings of men were all but alien to it.

'And what have I to do with Zingara, or Zingara with me?' asked Thoth-Amon.

Menkara opened his mouth, but Zarono decided that it was time to assert himself. With a boldness that he did not truly feel, he stepped forward, dropped to one knee before the throne, and drew from his doublet the parchment scroll that was Villagro's letter. This he handed to Thoth-Amon, who took it with his copper-ringed hand and dropped it in his lap.

'Mightiest of magicians,' he began, 'I bring you familial greeting from the lord duke of Kordava, who salutes you and offers rich gifts in return for some slight service, which this missive will explain.'

Thoth-Amon did not unroll the letter; he seemed to know its contents already. He mused for a time.

' 'Twere near to my heart to trample the accursed cult of Mitra into the slime and raise up the worship of our Father Set,' he murmured. 'But I am occupied with mighty magical operations, and Villagro's gold means little to me.'

'That is not all, dread lord,' said Menkara, drawing the *Book of Skelos* from under his robe. 'In tender of the duke's good will, we beg you to receive this gift from our hands.' He laid the ancient tome at Thoth-Amon's feet.

Thoth-Amon snapped his fingers, and the book rose into the air and settled gently, open, on the sorcerer's lap. The wizard-priest idly turned a few pages.

'A rare gift, in sooth,' he said. 'I had not thought a third copy yet existed; or have you rifled the royal librarium of Aquilonia?'

'Nay, dread lord,' quoth Menkara. 'A chance find, this, on the Nameless Isle that lies in the western sea . . .'

His voice trailed off, for the figure of the somber giant before them had suddenly grown tense. Cold fires leapt up in those snaky black eyes. The air seemed cold, and a sense of peril sprang up in Zarono. He caught his breath; had they done something to anger the great magician?

'Bore you away aught else from the altar of Tsathog-gua the Toad-god?' said Thoth-Amon in a soft voice like a sword sliding from its sheath.

Menkara quailed. 'Naught else, dread lord, save a sack or two of gems . . .'

'Which lay before the altar upon the book, did they not?'

Menkara nodded, trembling.

Thoth-Amon rose to his feet, and hellish fires blazed in his black eyes. The room seemed to blaze with green fire, and the pavement quaked as at the step of a giant. The magician spoke in a voice of thunder:

'You crawling worms! By such fools am I, Thoth-Amon, served! Set, mighty father, give me men of keener wit for slaves! *Ai kan-phog, yaa!*'

'Mighty one! Prince of magicians! How have we angered you?' wailed Menkara, groveling.

The grim gaze of the mighty Stygian swept down upon the pair in deadly wrath. His thunderous voice sank to a serpent's hiss.

'Know, fools, that there was hidden *beneath* the idol that whose worth the entire wealth of the earth cannot equal, compared to which the *Book of Skelos* is worth no more than a shopkeeper's tally sheet! I speak of the *Cobra Crown!*'

Zarono gasped. He had dimly heard of this sacred talisman of the serpent-men of Valusia – the most potent sorcerous sigil the earth had ever borne – the all-commanding crown of the serpent-kings, wherewith they had, in pre-human ages, gained the empire of the earth. And they had taken the book and the gems, leaving the supreme treasure behind!

Chapter 9

WIND IN THE RIGGING

For DAYS, the *Wastrel* lay becalmed off the Nameless Isle. The men sat along the rail, dangling fishing lines in the water. Half a cable's length forward of the ship, the crew of the longboat, belayed by a line to the *Wastrel's* bow, sweated at their oars, towing the carack inch by inch toward the unknown shores of the main continent.

Conan cursed and called upon his savage Cimmerian gods, but in vain. Day after day, the sails hung slack from their yards. The small, smooth swells slapped listlessly against the hull. To the south, thunderheads rose slowly into the hazy sky, and lightning flickered along the horizon at night; but where the *Wastrel* lay, the air was still.

The burly Cimmerian worried. Zarono's ship could have fallen upon him and taken him, except that the local calm would have halted the *Petrel* as surely as it had Conan's vessel. Either the Zingaran, too, lay becalmed over the horizon, or he had taken another route in departing from the island and so had missed the *Wastrel*.

Whatever errand of mischief Zarono was bound on, Conan thought, it was just as well that they had not fallen in with him. They had enough trouble of their own, without his help. For one thing, they were running low on food and fresh water.

For another, there was Sigurd and his crew. Conan had taken a liking to the frank, fearless young redbeard from Vanaheim and had offered berths among his own men to the marooned Barachans. He had known that this might lead to trouble, and so it had. There was fierce rivalry between the buccaneers of Zingara and the pirates – mainly Argosseans – of the Isles. Each had fought the other too often and too savagely to develop any mutual liking on short order.

Yet seamen are seamen and follow a common trade.

78

Ruthless though he was in many things, Conan felt that he could not simply up-anchor and sail away, leaving fellow mariners to their fate. So he had trusted that, between himself and Sigurd, they could keep the peace. Such, alas, had not been the case. The Zingarans had baited the hapless maroons until fighting broke out. No matter how often Conan or Sigurd hauled snarling sea dogs apart and beat sense into them, another fight was soon a-brewing.

This accursed calm aggravated the friction between the rival groups of corsairs. Furious with frustration, Conan growled a curse and gripped the rail between clenched hands. If ever, he hoped, a blessed wind would arise and give his men proper seamen's tasks to do, they would be too busy to spend time baiting rivals.

Another problem gnawed at his mind as well. Chabela had confided to him all that she had learned from Zarono and his snake-eyed Stygian sorcerer. Some information they had let slip, more she had overheard, and yet more she had shrewdly inferred, about the reason for Zarono's voyage and his seizure of her vessel. Much of the truth of the plot against the crown had revealed itself to her active mind, and all this she had passed on to Conan.

Now the Cimmerian was in a dilemma. A mere buccaneer, the dynastic conflicts of kingdoms meant little to him, and he owed little to Ferdrugo of Zingara. True, the old monarch had given him a royal commission as a privateer of the crown, and Kordava provided Conan with a safe harbor after voyages. But this much he might expect from any king of Zingara. The next one, in fact, might demand a smaller percentage of his loot.

In such matters, however, the rude chivalry of his Cimmerian heritage sometimes overcame his self-interest. It was not in the grim barbarian to stand idly by, ignoring the pleas of a beautiful Zingaran princess, while her royal father was slowly done to death by cunning plots and Stygian sorcery. Although he knew not what he was getting into, Conan at length decided to make her battle his own.

It was not, however, entirely altruism that suggested this course to the buccaneer. He had his ambitions, too.

He did not intend to remain a mere privateer all his days. If he could save the king of Zingara and his daughter from the plots of traitors and thus bolster the tottering throne, what could he not ask as a reward? A dukedom? An admiralship?

Conan even toyed with the idea of suing for Princess Chabela's hand and settling down as a royal consort. During a life of wild adventure, many women had tendered Conan the ultimate hospitality. But, although the Cimmerian treated women with a rough chivalry, he had avoided any kind of legitimate marriage. He liked to fulfill his definite obligations; and, to one whose lifeblood had been travel, adventure, and conflict, the thought of being tied down to one heart, with the welfare of a family to think of, was repugnant.

Now, however, he was over thirty-five and past the first flush of youth. Although he showed few signs of age save the many scars that crisscrossed his mighty frame, he knew that he could not expect to continue his footloose, brawling, roistering life forever. He would have to give some thought to his own future. Chabela was a fine, round, bouncing girl, forceful and intelligent, and she seemed to like him. He could fare further and do worse . . .

Frowning in thought, Conan left the rail, descended leisurely to his cabin, and flung himself into a chair. The twinkle of gems caught his eye, and he grinned sourly. Something, at least, had been gained from his efforts. On the desk before him, the Cobra Crown twinkled and flashed as the level shafts of the ruddy afternoon sun, slanting through the porthole, struck fire from its blazing gems.

On their march back from the cliff whence the toad-idol had fallen, Conan and his companions had again passed the black temple. Now, it seemed, the aura of evil, which had earlier enshrouded the ruin, was dispelled. The cryptic structure of black stone lay bathed in sparkling sunlight. No longer did an eery thrill of supernatural premonition tingle in the nerves of those who viewed it.

Cautiously, Conan set foot in the gloomy place again. Where the toad-god had squatted for untold ages, a black hole yawned in the plinth on which it had been enthroned. As Conan leaned over the cavity, his alert eye had caught the sparkle of gems. Had Zarono missed something? Conan quickly thrust his hand into the opening and brought forth the Cobra Crown.

It was a hollow cone of gold, crusted with thousands of white, fiery gems. Conan guessed these to be cut and faceted diamonds, although the craft of cutting and polishing the hardest of all gems was virtually unknown to the gem carvers of his day. The crown was fashioned into the likeness of a serpent, whose coils formed the conical headpiece and whose arched neck rose up from behind, to curve across the top of the crown so that the serpent's blunt head stared out above the brows of the wearer. Thousands of gems encrusted the Cobra Crown, and their worth was beyond calculation. So after all, the trip to the Nameless Isle had not been without its profit.

A roar of excitement roused the buccaneer from his somber thought: 'By Frigga's teats and Shaitan's fiery member!'

Conan grinned, knowing the voice of Sigurd the Vanr. An instant later, a red-bearded face, flushed with excitement, thrust into his doorway. Before either could speak, Conan knew the cause without words. The boom of taut canvas and the song of wind in the rigging came to his ears, and the cabin tilted as the ship heeled. The wind had come at last.

And what a wind! For two days and a night the *Wastrel*, stripped to a storm foresail, rode the scudding waves, driven by one of the lusty simooms that caused the mariners of the Hyborian Age to avoid these uncharted seas.

When the wind fell, the *Wastrel* dropped anchor in a cove on the coast of the main continent. Just where on the coast, Conan did not know, because a heavy overcast had hidden the sun and the stars during this leg of their voyage. Conan knew that they had sailed in a generally easterly direction. From the jungled appearance of the coast, he knew that they were south of the meadowlands of Shem; but whether they had made a landfall in Stygia, or in the kingdom of Kush, or in the little-known black countries still further south, remained to be seen.

'A chancy-looking place, my Captain,' grumbled Zeltran the mate. 'Where is it we might be?'

'The devil knows and the devil cares,' grunted Conan. 'The main thing is to find water; the butts are nigh empty and full of slime. Pick me a landing party, and let's be out with barrels. Jump to it!'

Zeltran scurried to the main deck to summon all hands. As the party assembled and swung down on lines to the longboat, Sigurd cast a frowning glance at the shoreline and grumbled one of his cosmopolitan curses. The Vanr had belted a huge leathern baldric across his matted chest.

'What's that, man?' demanded Conan.

Sigurd shrugged. 'Maybe naught, shipmate; but this land looks uncommon like the coasts of Kush.'

'Well, what of it? We were bound to hit Kush if we kept on to eastward.'

'If so it be, these lands are no safe haven for honest mariners. The black devils would as lief eat a man as give him the time of day. And there's tales of a nation of warrior women in the interior, fiercer fighters than the men even.'

Conan stared across the water to where the longboat labored shoreward. 'Maybe so, but water we must have, and our victuals are none too ample. When our stores are full, we'll steer north for Kordava again.'

Chapter 10

THE BLACK COAST

THE HARBOR into which they had sailed lay at the mouth of a small, sluggish river, whose banks were thickly grown with tall, slender palms and heavy underbrush. The longboat slowed in the shallows, and several buccaneers clambered overboard to drag it to safety higher up on the beach. Then, while archers mounted guard, the party trooped up the beach to the river mouth with empty casks. They continued on up the banks of the river, out of sight, stopping betimes to taste the water to see if they had reached the place where it was no longer brackish.

Conan, who had come ashore with the second boat-load, stood frowning on the beach with mighty arms folded on his bare chest. The configuration of the river mouth seemed naggingly familiar, and the name of the Zikamba River came unbidden to his mind. Either he had once seen this stretch of coast depicted on a chart, or he had actually touched here during his voyages with Belit, years before. The expression on Conan's grim, scarred features softened as he thought of his years with Belit at his side and a horde of howling black corsairs at his back. Belit – languorous, tawny panther of a woman – Belit whose eyes were like dark stars – his first and greatest love . . .

With the swiftness of a tropical storm, a screaming mob of naked blacks burst from the underbrush, their ebony bodies gleaming through beads, plumes, and war paint. Scraps of wild-animal skin girded their loins, and their hands brandished feather-tufted spears.

With a startled oath, Conan sprang from his resting place, whipping out his cutlass with a rasp of steel on leather and bellowing:

'To me, you buccaneer dogs! To arms! To me, and yare!'

The leader of the black warriors was a giant, muscled

like a statue of a gladiator hewn from gleaming black marble. Like the rest, he was naked but for a leopard-skin loincloth and a few beads and bangles. A crown of aigrettes nodded above his head. Intelligent black eyes looked out of a clean-lined face of majestic dignity.

In fact, to Conan's hasty glance, he looked oddly familiar. But Conan was too busy to search his memory. He sprinted up the slope of the beach, the sun flashing on the blade of his cutlass, to stand before his swiftly gathering crew and face the pelting charge of the black warriors.

Suddenly the plumed warrior in the lead halted, threw out his long, powerful arms, and bellowed: 'Simamani, wote!'

This command brought the charging mob to a halt – all but one man, who lunged past the leader, whipped back his arm, and started to hurl a keen-bladed assegai at Conan. His arm had started to lash forward when, moving with the speed of a striking adder, the leader brought his hardwood *kirri* smashing down on the warrior's head. The victim sprawled on the yellow sand, out cold.

Conan shouted to his men to hold their attack. For a long moment the two groups of armed men confronted each other, with javelins poised and arrows nocked. Conan and the black giant stood panting, face to face in taut silence. Then the black war chief's white teeth flashed in a grin.

'Conan!' he said in the Hyrkanian tongue, 'Have you forgotten an old comrade?'

As the other spoke, Conan's memory awoke. 'Juma! By Crom and Mitra, Juma!' he roared.

Dropping his cutlass, he sprang forward to hug the laughing black in his powerful arms. The buccaneers looked on in amazement as the two giants stood toe to toe, thwacking each other on the back and arms and shoulders with affectionate slaps and punches.

Years before, Conan had served in the legions of King Yildiz of Turan, far to the east. Juma the Kushite had been a fellow-mercenary. They had served together on an ill-fated expedition to farther Hyrkania, as escort for one of King Yildiz's daughters on her way to wed a nomad princeling of the steppes.

'Do you remember that fight in the snows of the Talakmas?' demanded Juma. 'And that ugly little god-king, what was his name? Jalung Thongpa or something.'*

'Aye! And the way that ugly green idol of the demon-king Yama, as tall as a house, came to life and squashed his only begotten son like a bug!' Conan replied with gusto. 'Crom, those were good days! But what in the name of nine scarlet hells are you doing here? And how did you become leader of these warriors?'

Juma laughed. 'Where should a black warrior be, if not on the Black Coast? And where should a born Kushite go home to, if not to Kush? But I could ask the same of you, Conan. Since when did you become a pirate?'

Conan shrugged. 'A man must live. Besides, I am no pirate, but a lawful privateer with letters of marque from the crown of Zingara. Not that – ahem – there's much difference between the two, come to think of it. But tell me of your adventures. How came you to leave Turan?'

'I am used to savanna and jungle, Conan; no native of the frozen North like you. Among other things, I got tired of freezing off my privates every Turanian winter.

'Besides, once you had drifted west, there were no more adventures. I had a hankering to see a palm tree once again and to tumble a plump black wench under the hibiscus bushes. So I resigned my commission, drifted south to the black kingdoms, and became a king myself!'

'King, eh?' grunted Conan. 'King of what? I didn't know there was anything down here but bands of bare-arsed savages.'

A mischievous grin lighted Juma's ebony features.
'That's what they are – or, at least, that's what they were before Juma came to teach them the arts of civilized war.' Juma turned his head and spoke to his men, who were fidgeting behind him as their leader conversed with the strange chief in a language they did not understand. '*Rahisi!*'

The Negroes relaxed and sat down on the sand where

* See 'The City of Skulls' in *Conan*, by Robert E. Howard, L. Sprague de Camp, and Lin Carter; Lancer Books, 1967.

they stood. Behind Conan, the buccaneers sat down, likewise, though keeping a wary eye on the blacks. Juma resumed:

'I found my birth-tribe engaged in an old feud with a neighboring tribe. We conquered the other tribe and absorbed it, and I became war chief. Then we conquered two other tribes, and I became war prince. Now I am ruler of all this coast for fifty leagues, and we are on the way to becoming a nation. I even plan to build a proper capital city, when I get around to it.'

'Hell's blood!' said Conan. 'You've learned more from this so-called civilization than ever have I. At least, you've risen further in the world. Good luck to you! When your bully-boys came charging out of the brush, I thought the gods had tired of playing with us and were going to sweep us off the board to lay down a new set of pieces. We landed here for water, as we have just lain becalmed off a damned island full of ghost snakes and walking statues.'

'You shall have enough water to float your ship in,' Juma promised, 'and once you have taken aboard all you need, you shall all be my guests at my village this night. We'll have a feast that will leave you staggering. I have a new crop of banana wine that ought to satisfy even your thirst!'

That night, most of Conan's crew sprawled on rattan mats in Juma's village of Kulalo, leaving a skeleton crew aboard the *Wastrel*. Kulalo – actually a sizable town – was a triple ring of conical huts of bamboo and thatch, sheltered behind a tall palisade and a thorn-bush boma.

A huge pit was dug in the open space at the heart of the town. This pit was filled with firewood and bracketed with huge spits, on which beeves, pigs, and antelope turned sizzling. Carved wooden bowls of sweetish, deceptively bland-tasting banana wine were passed from hand to hand. While black musicians beat drums in complex rhythms, fingered flutes, and plucked native lyres, young black women, clad only in a few beads and bangles, danced before the orange flames, clapping hands and shouting in chorus as they performed elaborate evolutions that would not have disgraced an emperor's troupe of dancing girls. The sailors gorged on wild pig,

86

Conan's feet. The care that the buccaneer captain took of it suggested that it contained something of value.

Bwatu carefully noted which hut Conan had retired to. As the feast roared on under the glory of the tropical moon, he rose to his own feet, stumbled as if drunken – albeit he was practically sober – and wandered off into the shadows. As soon as he was out of sight, he doubled back through the inky alleyways between the huts. A vagrant ray of moonlight flashed on the keen blade of his dagger – a dagger he had just received from a sailor for the use of one of his women.

Far to the north, in the Oasis of Khajar in Stygia, Thoth-Amon had for hours searched the astral plane for some token of the whereabouts of the precious relic of the serpent-men of ago-lost Valusia. While Menkara and Zarono slept in alcoves beyond the sanctum of his private laboratorium, the mighty Stygian at length perceived the hopelessness of his task. He sat motionless, his black gaze brooding on nothingness.

Shadows flowed and flickered within the great orb of crystal, which invisible hands had placed before his seat of power. Dim, wavering radiance, cast by moving figures within the crystal, sent shadows rippling across the sculptured walls of the chamber.

Thoth-Amon had established that the Cobra Crown no longer rested in its ancient hiding-place beneath the stone idol of Tsathoggua the toad-god. Only another party of mariners, landing by accident or design on the Nameless Isle, could have borne off the Crown. By the power of his crystal, Thoth-Amon had searched the island, foot by foot. Not only was the Crown gone; no human beings remained on the island. There was no sign of the Zingaran princess, of whose escape from the *Wastrel* Zarono had told him. The disappearance of the Crown and of Chabela, as well as the destruction of the idol, all pointed to the intervention by some party unknown.

The silence remained unbroken in the chamber. Shadows flickered across the walls and across the figure that sat on the throne, as motionless as if it, too, had been carved from stone.

Chapter 11

WEB OF DOOM

SELDOM WAS Conan of Cimmeria caught napping, but this was one of the times. The mild-tasting but heady beverage sent him into a deep slumber until, belatedly, his primitive sense of danger roused him. Slowly he came awake, foggily aware that something was wrong. For a moment he could not tell what had disturbed him.

Then he knew. A long slit had been cut in the woven reeds which composed the sides of the hut. The slit ran from man-height to the ground, and through the rent the cool night air blew across his sweating body.

Conan reached out and felt for the bundle that he had left lying at his side. Then, with a curse, he lurched to his feet and peered into the gloom around the hut. The Cobra Crown was gone.

Red fury boiled in Conan's heart; his bellow of rage shook the flimsy walls of the hut. Ripping out his cutlass, he charged out of the hut, cursing sulphurously.

The feast was still in progress for those few warriors still able to stand. The huge fire had burned low. Stars blazed like clustered gems above the nodding palms, and a nearly full moon showed her silver shield. Among the few who were still awake, Conan spied Juma and Sigurd. His shout brought them to their feet.

In swift words, he told what had happened. Since the crown was the only loot they had gathered during this voyage, Conan was stung to roaring rage by his loss.

All the buccaneers were accounted for, although few were conscious. A swift check of the folk of Kulalo, however, revealed that one was missing.

'Bwatu! Damballah singe his black soul!' Juma choked wrathfully, furious that one of his own people should have robbed his guest.

'You know the black dog?' roared Conan, too mad with rage to watch his tongue. Juma merely nodded grimly, describing the culprit.

'That surly-looking ugly you knocked sprawling back on the beach?' Conan demanded.

'The same. I guess he bore us both a grudge.'

'Or spotted the gems in the bag!' Sigurd commented. 'What's to do? Any idea where the rogue might hide, King Juma? By the bowels of Ahriman and the fiery claws of Shaitan, we should be after him ere he gets more of a start!'

'He would probably make for the land of our enemies, the Matamba.' Juma pointed northeast. 'Further north, Bwatu might fall into the path of the Ghanata slavers, who have been active in these parts of late. He could not, on the other hand, go very far southeast, for thither lies—'

To stand idly by while Juma calmly considered alternatives, while a fabulous fortune was borne ever farther away through the jungle night, was more than the fuming Conan could endure. Abruptly, he broke in on Juma's ponderings.

'Jaw all night, if you will!' he growled. 'Where's the trail to the land of the Matamba?'

'The path out the East Gate forks, and the trail leads northeast—'

Without waiting to hear the rest, Conan charged off toward his hut. On the way, he paused to pick up a water pot and empty it over his head. He came up blowing like a beached sea monster, but his skull ceased to throb and his wits began to clear.

When he raked the black mane of his hair out of his eyes, he saw Chabela, wrapped in a blanket, staring at him from her hut. 'Captain Conan!' she called. 'What has happened? Is the town attacked?'

He shook his head. 'Nothing, girl. Only a princely ransom in cut diamonds, thieved from me as I snored. Back to your pallet and be quick about it!'

Sigurd came puffing up. 'Lion!' he said. 'Juma and his headmen are trying to rouse the fleetest warriors. Don't start out by yourself into this jungle. The gods know what prowling beasts may be out there, so wait for Juma—'

'Be damned to the lot of you!' snarled Conan, whose eyes burned like those of a hunting beast. 'I am for

91

Bwatu before his trail grows cold, and Crom pity the jungle beast that gets in my way tonight!'

Without further speech, he was off. Like a charging buffalo, he ran for the East Gate and vanished from view.

'Damned Cimmerian temper!' swore Sigurd. He threw an apologetic glance at the princess and flung himself into the darkness after his comrade, calling out: 'Wait for me! Do not try it alone!'

The village was in an uproar. Juma and his chieftains strode among the sleepers, kicking them awake, hauling them to their feet, and bellowing commands.

Thus no eye noted as Chabela slipped back into her hut to don the rough garb with which Conan had furnished her out of the ship's slop chest. Gliding forth again, breeched and booted and armed, she slid into the shadows and quietly made her way to the East Gate.

'If the drunken oaf thinks he can order a royal princess of the House of Ramiro around . . .' she whispered angrily to herself.

There was, however, another and more compelling reason, besides her pique at Conan's brusque commands, that led her to leave Kulalo and set out alone after Conan. For all his roughness, he had treated her well and protected her. When he promised to return her unharmed to her father, he seemed really to mean it. Hence she felt that she could trust him much further than she could either his piratical crew or Juma's horde of black barbarians. With this in mind, she faded into the jungle, where the snarl of a hunting leopard echoed through the darkness.

Hours passed as Conan's furious rush carried him several leagues along the trail to Matambaland, leaving Sigurd far behind. When he paused for breath, he considered waiting for the pirate to catch up with him. But then the thought that any pause would let the wily Kushite get even further out of reach of his revenge sent him plunging along the trail with renewed vigor.

Conan knew the Kushite jungles well from that period, a decade earlier, when for a time he had been war chief of the Bamula tribe, further north. Where a less experienced man might think that to venture into the jungle alone was to hurl oneself into the maw of peril, Conan knew better. The great cats, for example, are cunning hunters but not particularly brave. Few will challenge a man alone unless starved or too old and lame to bring down fleeter prey. The very noise that Conan made, pounding along the winding trail, was his best assurance of safety.

The jungle, true, harbored other beasts, some more dangerous than the cats: the hulking gorilla, the blundering rhinoceros, the burly buffalo, and the mountainous elephant. Being plant eaters, all would usually leave men alone if given a wide enough berth, but if startled or crowded were likely to charge. Luckily, Conan encountered none of these in his pursuit of Bwatu.

As the sky lightened with the approach of dawn, Conan flung himself down to drink from a water hole and to bathe his chest and arms. Thorns and spines had tattered his white blouse and had drawn scarlet scratches across his chest and arms, until his torso streamed with mud, blood, and sweat.

Cursing, he wiped the back of his hand across his eyes, tossed back his black mane, and rested for a moment. Then, growling an oath, he rose and plunged grimly on, trusting to his iron strength. He had tested his endurance many times, in the course of his years of wild adventure, and he knew that he could outlast any common man, even one of the most powerful.

The sun rose over the jungle of Kush and lit a steamy, humid morning. The great cats retired, with bellies full or empty as the case might be, to sleep away the heat of the day.

By the growing light, Conan could see, where the trail was muddy, the fresh prints of long, splayed, bare feet. This, he was sure, was the spoor of the fleeing Bwatu. Although the run that Conan had already made would have caused most men to collapse, the sight of these tracks lent extra strength to his limbs.

Soon enough, Chabela regretted her impulsive action in following Conan into the forest. Conan and Sigurd, neither of whom knew that she was following them, soon out-distanced her. At a bend in the trail, she strayed off the path and at once lost all sense of direction. With the setting of the moon, the jungle had become as black as pitch. Beneath the canopy of leaves, she could not see the stars to get a hint of her direction. She wandered helplessly in circles, bumping into trees and tripping over roots and underbrush.

The night was alive with the chirp and click and buzz of nocturnal insects. Although Chabela feared the wild beasts, she encountered none. But now and then a distant rustle or the crashing of a large body through the brush brought her heart into her mouth.

Toward dawn, trembling with fear and fatigue, the exhausted girl sank down in a mossy glade to rest. Why had she ever done so foolish a thing as to rush off into this trackless maze? Worn out, she presently fell asleep.

She awoke in terror as strong black arms seized her and hauled her to her feet. She was surrounded by lean black men in ragged robes and turbans. They lashed her arms behind her and muffled her screams with a gag.

Toward mid-morn, Conan caught up with Bwatu, as he had known that he would. Bwatu, however, was in no state to return the stolen crown to Conan. He was dead – and empty-handed.

The thieving black lay face down on the trail in a puddle of blood. He had been virtually hacked to pieces. Conan squatted over the body and examined the wounds. These seemed to have been made by the blades of steel swords, not by the bronze or flint or ivory points of the native spears. Weapons of bronze and copper are easily dulled and notched by use and hence tend to leave ragged wounds, but these were the clean cuts typical of well-honed steel. The black folk of the Kushite jungles knew not the arts of smelting and forging ferrous metal. Hence iron and steel were rarities this far south, being found only when brought down by trade from the more advanced peoples to the north: the kingdom of Kush, properly so called, and Darfar and Keshan.

Conan wondered if the black Amazons had struck down the thief and carried off the crown, thus robbing him both of his property and his revenge. As he rose frm his crouch, lips drawn back in a snarl, a weighted net fell upon him from the branches above. Its thick strands enwrapped and pinned his limbs. With a roar of rage, the Cimmerian struck out with his cutlass, but the tough fabric yielded to the blow and closed all the tighter about him.

Like the web of some enormous spider, the net dragged him down and muffled his blows. The robed and turbaned blacks who rose from concealment beside the trail, in a calm and businesslike manner, drew tight the lead lines that tightened the net about Conan like the cocoon of some giant caterpillar. Other men dropped from the branches overhead and quickly clubbed their captive into unconsciousness.

As he fell forward into blackness, the Cimmerian's final thought was to curse himself for a besotted fool. Not in years had he let himself be caught in such a simple trap, netted like a Kushite bush pig. But it was too late for regrets now . . .

Chapter 12

CITY OF WARRIOR WOMEN

IN THE Oasis of Khajar, it was pitch-black night. A heavy blanket of cloud overlay the desert, shutting off the rays of the moon, which manifested themselves only as a faint, gray luminescence filtering through the clouds.

It was dark, too, in the throne room of Thoth-Amon. The green flames in the torcheres had dimmed to a mere glow, like that of fireflies. The Stygian sorcerer seemed to slumber on his carven chair, so motionless was he. Had any been present to observe, they would have seen that his muscular chest did not rise and fall. His grim visage was inert and vacant, like an inanimate mask. His body seemed untenanted.

And so it was. Failing to find any clues to the Cobra Crown on the astral plane, Thoth-Amon had freed his *ka* from its prison of flesh and ascended to the highest plane, the akashic. Here, in this dim, immaterial, spirit realm, the laws of time do not obtain. Past, present, and even a cloudy vision of the future lie visible to the all-encompassing glance of the adept, like a four-dimensional map. And here, in a sense, Thoth-Amon's spirit self could 'see' the arrival of the *Petrel*, the landing of Conan, the awakening of the toad-god, its destruction, the seizure of the Cobra Crown, and Conan's subsequent voyage to the Black Coast. That much Thoth-Amon observed before permitting his *ka* to descend again to the lower planes of the cosmos. The *ka* had to return before it altogether lost its connection with its material body.

So Thoth-Amon, reentering his body, felt a prickling sensation spread through his form as numb flesh again became animate. The sensation was like the familiar 'pins and needles' when circulation in a limb is inter-rupted; but, in the case of the prince of magicians, the tingling spread through his entire body. He stoically endured the pain. Then—

'Zarono! Menkara!' Thoth-Amon's voice rolled like thunder through the crypts beneath his palace.

'Eh?' said Zarono, pulling on his doublet as he came from his sleeping chamber, yawning and rubbing his eyes. 'What is it, my lord wizard?' Behind him, Menkara glided silently in.

'Prepare to return to the Black Coast at once. I have discovered the current whereabouts of the Cobra Crown and of your Princess Chabela. Both are in Kulalo, the capital of Juma the Kushite.'

'How got they there?' said Zarono.

'Your fellow ruffian, Conan the Cimmerian, took them—'

'That damned barbarian!' snarled Zarono. 'I'll—'

'If you encounter him, do to him as you will. I have no love for him, for he has caused me no small annoyance by his adventurings. But your main task will be to recapture your princess. Even I cannot control her mind at so great a distance.'

'And the Crown?'

'You may leave the Crown to me.'

'Are you coming with us, sir?'

Thoth-Amon smiled bleakly. 'Nay, not in the flesh. It will require a work of magic that few magicians in the entire world could do, and that will tax my powers to the utmost; but I shall reach Kulalo before you. Waste no time, you two, but gather your gear to set forth at once. Wait not even for daybreak!'

Conan revived in a vile temper. His head ached, as much from overindulgence in Juma's banana liquor as from having been beaten unconscious. Moreover, he was a disarmed and helpless captive, in the hands of slavers. Although this had happened to Conan before, it never failed to rouse him to a state of wild-beast fury.

Hours had passed, to judge by the angle of the sun's rays as they sent an occasional spear of light down through the roof of leaves. From the condition of his arms and legs, which were scraped raw, the burly Cimmerian assumed that he had been dragged through the underbrush to the clearing in which he now found himself. Heavy manacles bound his wrists. Through the tangle of his disordered mane, he glared about him, noting the number, alertness, and positions of the guards.

He was startled to see Chabela, huddled whitefaced and frightened in a cluster of sad-looking blacks. He had no idea of how she had been captured. He did not, however, see Sigurd among the captives. This might or might not be a good thing.

Then, mounted on a lean mare, a tall black in the gray robes of a slaver cantered into the clearing. Like the other slavers, this man was black of skin, but lean and wiry, with sharper-cut features than were usual among the jungle tribes. Conan guessed that the slavers were Ghanatas, of whom Juma had already spoken. This was a nation of nomadic Negroes, who dwelt in the deserts along the southern borders of Stygia. While Shemite and Stygian slavers raided the Ghanatas and other peoples of Kush and Darfar for captives, the Ghanatas in turn raided still farther south, into the equatorial jungles.

The newcomer reined up and exchanged curt words with the man in command of the group that had captured Conan. The latter turned away, snapping his whip and yelling for his men to get the slaves moving.

The captives were herded into a double line. Their manacles were chained together so that no one of them could break free by himself. The giant Cimmerian towered above the surrounding blacks, bending a lion-like glare about him. The mounted slaver ran a cold, disdainful glance over the lot.

'By Zambi,' he grunted, and spat. 'This lot will scarcely bring a fistful of cowrie shells in Gamburu!'

His lieutenant nodded. 'Aye, Lord Mbonani. Methinks they grow feebler year by year. The breeding stock must be running out . . .'

Just then, a slaver flicked Conan on the shoulder with his whip. As the whip kissed his skin, the Cimmerian swung into action. Swifter than thought, he reached up with his manacled hands, caught the whip, and pulled with a mighty surge of power.

Jerked off balance, the slaver sprawled at Conan's feet. As the man scrambled up, snarling curses, he half drew the heavy, razor-edged Ghanata knife – really more a short sword – from its scabbard thrust through his girdle.

Before the weapon could clear its sheath, Conan kicked the slaver in the face, knocking him down again. Conan then bent, pulling the blacks chained next in line to him off their feet in turn, and seized the hilt of the knife. Another slaver raced toward Conan, whirling an ax up over his head to split the Cimmerian's skull. Before the blow could fall, Conan drove the knife to the hilt in the slaver's belly, so that the point stood out a hand's breadth from the man's back just above the kidneys.

As the slaver paled, gurgled, and collapsed, the clearing erupted into a whirling mass of yelling men. Chained as he was, Conan had no chance. Still, it took five men to hold him and three more to batter his thick skull with clubs until he again sagged to the ground, unconscious.

Mbonani, struggling to keep his frightened mare under control, watched the flurry of action with an appraising stare. 'Well,' he grunted, 'that one at least has spirit. A white man, too; what does he here?'

'I mentioned him earlier,' said the slaver lieutenant. 'There is a white woman, also – that one, yonder.' Mbonani looked Chabela over appraisingly.

'The two best of the lot,' he said. 'Treat them well, Zuru, or it will go hard with you.'

Mbonani walked his horse forward to where Conan, his face a mask of blood from scalp wounds, was dazedly lurching to his feet again. As Conan raised his bloody face, Mbonani struck the Cimmerian across the cheek with his riding whip.

'That for slaying one of my men, white man!' he barked.

The blow raised a welt, but the barbarian neither winced nor cried out. He watched the slaver captain with cold, expressionless hatred. Mbonani grinned wolfishly, showing white teeth against his black skin.

'I like your guts, white man!' he said. 'Keep them, so that the Amazons shall pay a good price. Now forward!'

Escorted by the ragged slavers, the double line of captives clanked along the trail to Gamburu.

Conan marched with the rest, his iron frame stolidly enduring the heat, the thirst, the flies, and the burning weight of the sun. He wondered what had befallen the Cobra Crown, but it was an idle thought. When one's life is at hazard, he had long since learned, loot becomes a mere side issue.

At length he noted a bulge in one of Zuru's saddle bags. Conan's eyes gleamed with savage humor. The slave lieutenant might bow and scrape before Captain Mbonani, but he obviously had a mind of his own.

The Ghanta slavers led their captives out of the jungle and into an area of grassy veldt. On the next day, gleaming in the low sun of the late afternoon, the stone city of Gamburu loomed on the horizon.

Conan stared at the city appraisingly. Compared to glittering Aghrapur, the capital of Turan – or even Meroe, the capital of the kingdom of Kush – Gamburu was not impressive. Still, in a land where most houses were squat cylinders of dried mud and thatch, and a city wall was a stockade of sharpened wooden poles, and a 'city' was but an overgrown village by the standards of more northerly lands, Gamburu stood out.

About the city ran a low wall of uncemented stone blocks, rising to about twice the height of a man. Four gates broke the circle of this wall, each flanked by guard towers with slits for archers and machicolations for the abuse of besiegers. Massive wooden valves were set in the gates.

Conan noted the masonry of the gates. Some of the stones were ordinary fieldstone, crudely chipped to fit. Others were finely dressed ashlars, but worn as if by great age. As Mbonani led his clanking column through the western gate, Conan observed that the houses inside the city showed a similar mixture. Most of the buildings were of one or two stories, with roofs of thatch. The lower story was in most cases made largely of old, well-carved stones, while the upper was composed more of newer and cruder masonry. Here and there a bit of sculpture, such as a frowning, demonic face, appeared on the surface of one of the worn old stones; but it was as often as not mounted in its wall sideways or upside down.

From his previous experience with ruined cities, Con-

an drew his own conclusions. Some ancient – perhaps
pre-human – folk had originally built a city here. Centuries later, the ancestors of the present inhabitants had
taken possession of the town. In building and rebuild-
ing, they had re-used the ancient stones and had also
imitated, though crudely, the stone-building methods
of their predecessors.

The hooves of Mbonani's mare kicked up little clouds
of dust from the unpaved streets and betimes splashed
through a mud puddle. As the column shambled along
the main street, the Gamburuvians crowded to the sides
to let them pass.

Conan's glance darted from side to side as he strode
along. He noted that, in this city, the sexes differed in
an unusual way. The women were tall and powerful;
they strode imperiously, like great black panthers, with
bronze swords slapping their naked thighs. They were
resplendent in bangles and beads, in plumes and lion-
skin headdresses.

The men, on the other hand, were puny, sad-looking
blacks, inches shorter than the women and confined to
such menial tasks as street-cleaning, chariot-driving, and
litter-bearing. Conan, tall even for a Cimmerian, towered
over them all.

The column crossed a bazaar, where merchandise lay
spread under awnings in the twilight, and thence down
a broad avenue to a central plaza. This huge open
space, a bowshot across, was fronted on one side by the
royal palace, a worn but imposing structure of dull-red
sandstone. On either side of the gate rose a pair of
massive, squat statues of the same material. They were
not the statues of human beings – that much was evident
from their proportions – but just what they were meant
to represent was hard to tell, so worn by the weather
of ages were they. They could have originally been
figures of owls, of apes, or of some unknown pre-human
monstrosities.

Conan's attention was next drawn to a peculiar pit
in the center of the plaza. This shallow depression was
a good hundred feet across. Its rim was cut down into
the earth in a series of concentric steps, like the rows of
stone benches in an amphitheater. The floor of the pit
was strewn with sand, in which stood a few puddles from

101

recent rains. In the midst of these sands rose a peculiar clump of trees.

Conan had never, in all his travels, seen an arena like this. He was, however, allowed only a momentary glimpse of it before he was hurried along to the slave pen. There he remained with his fellow captives through the night under heavy guard.

The one glimpse, however, had shown Conan a disquieting detail. Scattered about the bases of the strange-looking trees, white against the yellow-brown of the sand, was a clutter of clean white bones – human bones, such as one might find about the lair of a man-eating lion.

Conan thought about this oddity all the way to the pen. The Argosseans, he knew, sometimes fed condemned criminals to lions in their arena in Messantia; but such an arena was so planned that no lion could leap from the floor up into the tiers of benches where sat the spectators. This pit was too shallow for such a purpose; a lion could clear it in a single bound.

The more Conan thought about this phenomenon, the more uneasy he became.

Chapter 13

THE QUEEN OF THE AMAZONS

DAWN BROKE in orange flame above the squat stone towers of the city of the Amazons. The display did not long abide; for in these tropical latitudes, the sun soared almost straight up from the horizon. With dawn, Conan, Chabela, and the other new-caught slaves were herded from the pen and marched to the bazaar. Here, one by one, they were stripped, led to the block, displayed, bargained over, and finally led away.

The buyers were all women, who were the ruling sex in Gamburu. The tall, lean Mbonani stood to one side, his hawklike black face impassive, as the buyers haggled with his lieutenant Zuru. The warrior women accorded more respect to the Ghanatas, whose slave-catching talents they valued, than they did to their own men.

When Chabela's turn came, the girl blushed scarlet and tried to hide her person with her hands as she stood naked on the block. When Zuru had made her turn about, he shouted for bids.

'Five quills,' said a voice from a veiled litter.

Zuru glanced around the crowd of Gamburuvians and said: 'Sold!'

Since both had spoken in the bastard Ghanatan used as a trade language from the kingdom of Kush southward, Conan understood. He was surprised that such a low bid had not been topped. A 'quill' was a length of quill from the wing feathers of one of the larger birds, filled with a minute amount of gold dust; for the land of the Amazons had not yet learned the use of coined money. Still, Conan wondered why an aristocratic young beauty like Chabela had not fetched a higher price. The person in the litter must be so important that nobody dared bid against him – or her, Conan corrected himself.

He was tired, hungry, and in a vile temper. He had been clubbed until his scalp was a mass of wounds and swellings. He had been forced to walk leagues in the broiling sun, had been given precious little food or drink or sleep, and he was as touchy as a lion with a toothache. So, when one of the slavers jerked his chain to lead him to the block, he almost – but not quite – burst into violent and unthinking action.

A few years before, Conan would have laid lethal hands on the slaver and damned the consequences. But hard-won experience checked his impulse. He could undoubtedly kill this one guard, and perhaps several more before they brought him down, as they inevitably would. These were hardened marauders who had dealt with many a recalcitrant slave before. At ten paces, one of them could hurl a javelin through the ring made by a man's thumb and forefinger without touching his flesh.

If Conan attacked them, he might get a few, but the rest would stick him full of spears and hack him apart with their knives before he could fill his lungs to give a war cry. And then, who would care for Chabela? In taking on her cause, he had – he hated to admit it, even to himself – assumed a certain responsibility for her. He must live.

His eyelids narrowed to slits; his mouth was compressed to a thin gash; the veins in his temples throbbed and swelled with his suppressed fury. His limbs quivered with the effort of his self-control as he walked to the block. A nearby slaver mistook this tremor for a sign of fear and whispered as much to a comrade, smiling as he spoke. Conan sent the turbaned black a hard, level gaze that wiped the smile from his features.

'Strip, you!' snapped Zuru.

'You will have to help me off with these boots,' said Conan calmly. 'My feet are swollen from much walking.' He sat down on the block and held out one leg.

Zuru grunted and seized the boot. For an instant he wrestled vainly with it. Then Conan gently placed his other foot against the slaver's backside, relaxed the foot in the boot, and shoved. Zuru shot away as if hurled from a catapult, to fall face-down in a puddle.

With a scream of rage, the slaver lieutenant bounded to his feet. Snatching a whip from another slaver, Zuru ran back to where Conan sat with a faint smile on his grim features.

'I— I will teach you, white dog—' yelled Zuru, making a furious cut at Conan with the whip.

As the lash of hippopotamus hide snaked toward him, Conan shot out a hand and caught the whip. Then, still not rising from the block, he pulled the whip in, hand over hand, drawing Zuru toward himself.

'Be careful, little man,' he rumbled. 'You would not wish to damage your merchandise, now would you?'

The slaver chief, Mbonani, had been watching the scene. Trying to suppress a smile, he spoke: 'The white dog is right, Zuru. Let his new owner teach him manners, not you.'

But Zuru was too far gone in rage to heed even his captain. With an inarticulate howl, he whipped out his Ghanata knife. Conan rose to his feet, gathering the slack of the chain that connected his wrists to use as a weapon.

'Hold!' cried an imperious voice from the veiled litter. Its tone of command brought even the infuriated Zuru to a halt.

A jeweled black hand whipped aside the muslin hangings, which concealed the rider within from the eyes of the vulgar. A black woman stepped from the palanquin, and Conan's eyes widened with involuntary admiration.

The woman was well over six feet in height – almost as tall as Conan, and of robust build. Black as oiled ebony was she, and sunlight gleamed in satiny highlights on the curves of her heavy breasts, sleek thighs, and long, muscular legs. A jeweled coif in her bush of kinky black hair bore ostrich plumes dyed several brilliant colors: peach, rose, and emerald green. Uncut rubies gleamed in her ear lobes, and pearls shone softly in multiple strands about her neck. Bracelets of pure, soft gold jingled on her arms and ankles. Otherwise, her only garment was a brief kilt of leopard skin about her voluptuous loins.

Nzinga, queen of the Amazons, bent a lingering gaze upon the giant Cimmerian. Silence fell upon the bazaar. Slowly the queen's full lips parted in a languorous smile.

'Ten quills for the white giant,' she said at last.
There were no further bids.

Chabela found her new life as a slave almost unendurable. It was bad enough that she, who had been the pampered daughter of a powerful monarch, must now fetch and carry at the behest of a black queen. Worse yet was the fact that slaves were required to go about their tasks naked; garments were for free tribesmen only.

She slept on a verminous pallet in the slave quarters. A harsh-voiced, heavy-handed slave-mistress roused her and her companions in thralldom with the first light of dawn to cook and clean, scrub and mop, and serve at the royal table. It did her no good to see the erstwhile Zingaran buccaneer, Conan, lolling on fat cushions at these feasts, guzzling banana wine and gorging on fish cakes and pastries.

Her estimate of the redoubtable Cimmerian fell. She did not have a word equivalent to the modern 'gigolo,' but she knew the concept well enough. Her contempt for Conan was aggravated by the fact that he did not seem to resent his status as the queen's kept lover. No man worthy of the name, she told herself, would sink so low as to *enjoy* such disgusting servitude. Experience had not yet taught her, as it had long taught Conan, to accept such conditions as came one's way when one could do nothing to change them.

Since Conan was the only person in this dreadful city whom she could even consider as a friend, she would have despaired utterly, had not Conan, on a few rare occasions when nobody was looking, tipped her a broad wink. The wink said – or at least she hoped that it said – 'Keep up your courage, girl; I'll get you out of this yet.'

On the other hand, even Chabela was forced to admit that Queen Nzinga was a magnificent woman. The girl tried to imagine their behavior in bed; but, having been delicately reared, she lacked the worldly knowledge to do so. She could not know that, however the splendid black lioness of Gamburu might queen it in public, Conan was the master of the bedroom.

This was something new, too, for Queen Nzinga. Her experience, and the whole culture of her kingdom, assumed that woman was man's natural superior. A hundred queens had reigned before her on the Ivory Throne. Each of them had despised and degraded their men, using them as servants and as tools of pleasure and parenthood, and discarding them when they became sickly or exhausted or tiresome. Such had also been her way.

Until the giant Cimmerian had come into her life, she had easily dominated all her men. But Conan could not be dominated; his will was harder than iron, and he was even taller and stronger than she. In the clasp of his mighty arms, the black Amazon found pleasures beyond her previous experience. She became insatiable in her hungers.

She also became fiercely jealous of all the women whom the Cimmerian must have known before her. Of them, however, he would say nothing; her questions were ignored. Conan was not without a certain rude chivalry in such matters. Rail and bellow and smash things though she would, he remained unmoved, with a faint smile on his lips.

'And what of that plump little white wench the Ghanatas captured along with you?' Nzinga flared. 'She was your lover, yes? You found her soft, perfumed body desirable, did you not? More desirable than Nzinga, eh?'

Looking at her in the passion of her fury, with her eyes blazing and the ebon globes of her breasts dancing, Conan had to admit that never since his first great love, Belit of the Black Corsairs, had he known a more splendid woman. But, now that he knew she was jealous of Chabela, he must be careful – extremely careful. He must find some way to quench those suspicions, or Chabela would suffer. Nzinga was quite capable of ordering the head smitten off anyone, man or woman, who thwarted her.

Conan had hitherto done what little he could to lessen Chabela's misery. Now, however, he would not dare to intervene even to that small extent, lest Nzinga get wind of it.

He yawned. 'Chabela? I hardly know the child,' he said. 'She is a high-born Zingaran, and such folk place an absurdly high value on virginity. If I had loved her, she wouldn't be here now.'

'What mean you?'

'She'd have slain herself, as they are taught to do there.'

'I believe you not! You are trying to protect—'

Conan seized Nzinga in the grip of one mighty arm, bent her backwards into the nest of pillows, and drank furious kisses from her panting mouth. He knew that he could dare her temper just so far. In the present situation, there was only one treatment that he could count upon to take her mind off her jealous broodings . . .

Chapter 14

UNDER THE LASH

FOR SEVERAL days more, time passed without incident.
Then . . .

Nzinga lolled on cushions in her seraglio or private
quarters. For two days, the white slave, Chabela of
Zingara, had been assigned to the most exhausting and
degrading tasks. These chores were performed under
the very eye of Conan. Nzinga saw to this by a system
of carefully planned subterfuge and accident.

Wary of the queen's attention, Conan assumed a
mask of indifference, although he often boiled with a
rage to strike out on behalf of the captive princess.

Failing to draw any reaction from the Cimmerian,
the black queen staged a final scene calculated to expose
Conan's true feelings. She declared a small feast for
several of her Amazon officers – big, scarred, tough-
looking black women, with about as much femininity,
in Conan's eyes, as a battle ax.

During the feast, the Zingaran girl waited upon her
mistress and upon the latter's fancy man. As she was
serving wine, one of the Amazon officers shot out a
sandaled foot and tripped her.

With a stifled cry, Chabela lost her balance and
upset a beaker of wine over several feasters. One of
these, a stout officer named Tuta, scrambled to her
feet with a oath and struck the cowering slave girl a
terrific blow across the face with her open hand. The
girl sprawled on the earthen floor.

A sadistic gleam lit the eyes of the Amazon officer;
the sight of the cowering, naked white girl seemed to
rouse her to additional fury. In tingling silence, she
approached the slave girl like a panther stalking its
prey. One scarred, muscular hand sought a needle-sharp
bronzen dirk, which hung at her hip.

The room remained silent, save for the faint whisper
as the ruddy blade, gleaming in the torchlight, slid

from its sheath. Tuta, her face a mask of bloodlust, bent over the slave girl and raised the dagger.

With breathless fascination, Chabela watched the approach of the dirk. She knew that she ought to leap to her feet and run, even though she was sure to be caught. But the horror and hopelessness of her position drained the strength from her limbs, so that she could only stare helplessly. In another instant, the blade would sink into her panting breast . . .

Then Tuta froze as a viselike grip seized her by wrist and nape. The crushing pressure of those huge hands paralyzed her as surely as her approach had paralyzed Chabela. The dirk dropped to the ground with a faint, metallic sound. Then, with a surge of his powerful thews, Conan hurled her across the hall, to sprawl, half stunned, against the further wall.

Conan was fully awake to the position into which Nzinga had maneuvered him. He could not let the daughter of King Ferdrugo be stabbed to death; on the other hand, he realized that Nzinga would take his interference as proof of his interest in her rival and vent her jealousy on one or both of them. He forced a laugh.

'Surely the queen of Gamburu is not so spendthrift as to let her slaves be slain for a few drops of wine!' he said, grinning as jovially as he could.

Queen Nzinga eyed him coldly, without expression. Then she gave a small signal to Chabela, who scrambled up and scurried from the room. The tension relaxed. Conan returned to his place. Beakers of wine went round again, and desultory conversation sprang up.

Conan hoped that the taut moment was over. He covered his thoughts with deep drafts of plantain wine. But he did not fail to notice that Queen Nzinga was eyeing him from time to time with hard, thoughtful eyes.

As Chabela left the dining hall, powerful black hands seized her and held her fast. Before she could cry out, a wad of cloth was thrust into her mouth and secured by a strip of the same material tied around her face and the back of her neck. Then a sack of cloth was drawn

110

over her head. Her wrists were twisted behind her and bound with leather straps. She was lifted off her feet and borne through twisting corridors and down steps to an area of the palace that she did not know. Here her wrists were unbound but then bound again, above her head, to a copper ring suspended by a chain from the ceiling. When this was done, she was left alone.

The pain in her hands slowly diminished as the straps cut off the circulation in them, rendering them numb. She dangled weakly in the silent room, praying that Conan could somehow learn of her predicament.

But Conan, at this moment, was himself helpless. He sprawled on the cushions of the dining chamber. His eyes were closed, his head lay back, and he snored like distant thunder. Although he had drunk only moderately, a sudden lassitude had come upon him. The thought entered his bemused mind that perhaps Nzinga had drugged him – but, before he could do anything about it, he fell into a slumber so profound that not even an earthquake could have aroused him.

Nzinga gave him a slitted glance and tersely ordered him borne from the room. Then she arose to stalk through the corridors to the chamber where Chabela hung. As she strode, fury grew in her heart like the flames pent in a brazen furnace, and gloating anticipation smoldered in her fierce gaze.

The sack was snatched from Chabela's head and the gag from her jaws. She found herself looking into the blazing eyes and savage smile of Nzinga. The slave girl gave a cry of terror.

The black Amazon laughed. 'Scream all you like, you white-skinned milksop. It will avail you naught!'

As Chabela hung in her bonds, Nzinga ran a gloating gaze over her victim's supple body. The queen turned away and chose a whip from several instruments of torment that hung from hooks along the wall. The lash, six feet of supple hippopotamus hide from braided handle to threadlike tip, slithered across the floor like a crawling serpent. Chabela stared with horror. Again, the queen laughed harshly.

'Conan's lips have never thrilled you,' she said, 'as

will the kiss of my pet here. Nor have his hands caressed your flesh as shall the lash.'

'What have I ever done to you, that you should torment me so?'

'You took Conan's heart from me, ere we first met!' snarled Nzinga. 'Never have I known such a man. But his arms have crushed you in their embrace; his lips have rained burning kisses on your white bosom . . . These things I know, and I cannot bear the knowledge! With you gone, he will turn to me and love me with all his mighty heart. I will make him king in Gamburu – an office no male has held for a thousand years!' She swished the whip.

'It is not true!' moaned Chabela. 'Never has he touched me!'

'You lie! But the kiss of the lash shall wring the truth from you!'

Nzinga drew back her arm, and the lash sang and cracked about Chabela's waist. The girl screamed at the knifelike stab of agony. The whip left a scarlet weal, from which drops of blood slowly oozed.

Nzinga slowly drew back her arm for another slash. The only sound in the chamber was Chabela's hoarse breathing.

Again the whip sang, and a shriek of anguish was torn from the slave girl as the lash coiled about her loins. Nzinga watched, her handsome face distorted with eager lust, as the naked girl writhed and twisted in her bonds. Again she struck; now her ebony body glistened with tiny drops of sweat. Again Chabela screamed. The queen laughed, licking her full lips.

'Scream all you like, whimpering slave! No one can hear you. Even if he could, no one would dare to come to your aid. Conan lies in a drugged slumber, from which he will not recover for hours. In all the world, there is no one to help you!'

Her face alight with unholy passion, the giant Amazon caressed with her eyes the form of the slave, now glistening with sweat and blood, as she drew back her arm once more. She meant to indulge her perverted lust to the utmost, until the girl expired beneath the torture of the whip.

Never had Chabela imagined that flesh could endure such torment. Pampered by the luxuries of court life, the princess had never experienced true pain before. Added to the agony of her flesh was the torment of shame. As the only daughter of a fond old king, she had been allowed to go her headstrong way, rarely thwarted by her aged and preoccupied royal parent. Now, as her flesh shrank from the kiss of the lash, so did her spirit shrink from the humiliation.

The Zingaran nobility commonly held black slaves – Kushites brought up from the south by Stygian and Shemitish slavers – and Chabela knew that they were often punished for real or imagined faults just as she was being chastised now. But never in her wildest imaginings had she supposed that the roles could be reversed, and that a black woman could have her strung up and flog her like the meanest field hand on a Zingaran plantation.

As lash followed lash, Chabela, through the red haze of pain, fixed her gaze on a glittering object that lay across the chamber on a small taboret: a golden head-piece, crusted with countless gems, in the form of a coiled serpent. Of course! She recognized the Cobra Crown, which Conan had seized from the black temple on the Nameless Isle. She strove to keep her mind on the Crown, to counteract the pain of the flogging . . .

The Crown, she remembered vaguely, had been stolen from Conan in Kulalo – how long ago? Eons, it seemed. Then, how came it here? The slavers who had captured herself and Conan must have also taken the Crown from the thief who had stolen it originally.

Nzinga had paused in her work to gulp wine. Now she was returning to the scarlet rapture of the whip. Steeling herself for the next blow, Chabela forced her eyes open. Through her tangled locks, she beheld a baffling scene.

Behind the nearly naked Nzinga, a weird phenomenon was taking place. First came a faint luminescence – a phosphorescent shimmer of elusive radiance, like the will o' the wisp of a ghost-haunted swamp.

Then the faint green light brightened and expanded. Within the time of a dozen heartbeats, it assumed a spindle shape as tall as a man.

Chabela gasped. Observing that the girl was staring wide-eyed at something behind her, Nzinga whirled. As she did so, the spindle brightened to a blinding emerald flame, then faded and vanished. In its place stood a man.

This man was dusky of skin, tall, and powerful. He had a harsh bronze mask of a face, with keen black eyes and a jutting beak of a nose. His head had recently been shaved, so that his hair was a mere black stubble, so short that the brown scalp showed through it. He wore a simple white linen robe, which left his muscular arms bare.

Thoth-Amon looked older than when Zarono and Menkara had entered his presence in his underground throne room. Beads of sweat bedewed his swarthy forehead, for the magical operation that had transported him bodily from the Oasis of Khajar to Gamburu had been one of the most powerful known to the magical fraternity. Few wizards in the world were capable of it, and the mental effort had taxed even Thoth-Amon's powers to the utmost.

Nzinga was amazed that a stranger – and a contemptible male, at that – should come unannounced into her disciplinary chamber. The intrusion was an incredible affront, for which she instantly decided to have the stranger's head. She opened her mouth to shout for her guards, at the same time drawing back her arm for a slash of the whip.

The Stygian watched with a quiet, enigmatic smile on his somber face. As the whip rose, he extended a hand toward the black queen. A nimbus of jade-green radiance flickered into being about his fingers, brightened, and grew, until a beam of emerald light shot out to bathe in glory the ebony figure of Nzinga of Gamburu.

The queen uttered one harsh cry, tensed as if stabbed, and collapsed limply, to sprawl on the earthen floor. The ray faded and vanished.

Some premonition caused Chabela to slump as if unconscious, hanging from the straps that bound her wrists to the overhead ring. She let her head fall forward, so that her thick mass of glossy black hair obscured her features.

114

Thoth-Amon gave her scarcely a glance. She was obviously a slave being punished for some fault and hence beneath his notice. Never having seen Chabela at close range in the flesh, he did not realize that she was the princess whom Menkara and Zarono were hunting along the Black Coast. Wizards are as capable of blunders as common men.

When Thoth-Amon had sent his *ka* to the akashic plane, Conan and Chabela had still been in Kulalo; Bwatu had not yet stolen the Cobra Crown. At that time the future was too clouded by possible alternatives for the wizard to discern.

After his minions had departed on their expedition to recapture the princess, Thoth-Amon had recourse to his scry-stone again. He wished to locate the Cobra Crown accurately before undertaking the powerful spell that should transport him thither. Since he could remain at the far end of his journey only for a limited time, he could not afford to materialize at some point leagues distant from the thing that he sought.

In the meantime, however, Bwatu had stolen the Crown and had been slain by the slavers. Zuru had hidden the Crown and taken it with him to Gamburu, where Queen Nzinga had paid him enough quills of gold dust to make him wealthy for life. Hence, when Thoth-Amon sought to locate the Crown by crystallomancy, he had – somewhat to his surprise – discovered that it was no longer in Kulalo but in Gamburu.

About Conan and Chabela he did not concern himself. Chabela he assumed to be still in Kulalo, whence Zarono and Menkara would in due course remove her. In any case, the spell that transported him to Gamburu would not have enabled him to fetch another human being back to his lair with him.

As for Conan, Thoth-Amon regarded the Cimmerian buccaneer as but a minor annoyance, as one would a buzzing mosquito. If Conan got in his way, Thoth-Amon would swat him as one would an insect; but he would not go out of his way to pursue him. He was playing for bigger stakes than the life of a mere barbarian adventurer.

Had Thoth-Amon focused his occult vision on Chabela, he would soon have divined her identity. Just now, however, his whole attention was bent upon the Cobra Crown. A flicker of delight lit up his harsh features as he recognized the object on its taboret. Quickly he strode across the senseless body of the Amazon queen to where the Crown rested. With reverently caressing hands, he raised the Crown and examined it in the torchlight, running his strong brown fingers delicately over the curving coils and the great white jewels that studded them.

'At last!' he breathed, the fires of insatiable ambition leaping up in his dark eyes. 'With this, the empery of the world is within my grasp! And the holy rule of Father Set shall be restored over lands near and far!'

As a grim smile lit his normally impassive features, Thoth-Amon spoke a word of power and made a peculiar gesture. A whirling web of green light enshrouded his figure and lit it. The light faded, shrank to a mere spindle of green phosphorescence, and flickered out.

Left alone in the chamber with the recumbent body of the queen, Chabela roused herself from her stupor of horror and terror. By standing on tiptoe, she found, she could ease the pressure of the straps that bound her wrists to the ring overhead. Although the straps had been drawn tightly, her hands and wrists were now so covered with sweat that the bonds could be slid along them. She struggled, first with one arm and then the other. After an eternity of effort, one hand at last slipped free from its strap. The other quickly followed.

Exhausted, Chabela collapsed to the floor. Her hands were so numb that she could not even flex her fingers. Soon, however, red-hot needles of returning circulation began to stab into them. She whimpered with the pain but choked back the sound lest it rouse her enemy, the queen.

Little by little, sensation and control returned to Chabela's hands. She rose, staggering a little, and bent over the form of Nzinga. The queen's superb breasts rose and fell in regular breathing, as if she were in a normal sleep.

Chabela limped across the room to where stood the ewer of wine from which Nzinga had refreshed herself.

The princess drank the sweetish, bland liquid in thirsty gulps. New strength flowed into her limbs.

Then she turned her attention back to the unconscious queen. Chabela's eyes sought the dagger at Nzinga's girdle. Should she snatch it from its sheath and bury it in the queen's bosom? She trembled with hatred of the queen. She longed to slay her with a passion that she had never felt against any human being.

But she hesitated. For one thing, she had no way of knowing in how profound a slumber Nzinga lay. Suppose she drew the dagger. The motion might arouse the queen, who, being far larger and stronger than the sturdy little princess, would seize her arms and either slay her herself or shout for her guards to come and seize her. Even if Chabela possessed herself of the weapon without arousing her foe, her first stab must needs be instantly fatal. Otherwise the queen, at the very least, would cry out for help before she expired.

Another consideration also held her back. The code of chivalry of Zingara, with which she had been imbued since childhood, absolutely forbade the slaying of a sleeping foe. True, Zingarans violated their own rules quite as often as men of other nations did theirs; but Chabela had always tried to live up to the highest ideals of her race. If she could have slain the queen without danger to herself, she might have overcome her instinctive repugnance to such a treacherous act. As things were, however . . .

She quickly stole across the chamber and drew aside the hanging cloth that masked the doorway. Summoning up her courage, the girl stepped forward into the darkness.

In the chamber, the torches burned low, their ruddy light flickering on the empty ring that dangled from the ceiling, on the bloodstained whip, and on the sprawled black body of the queen.

Chapter 15

THE BLACK LABYRINTH

As she left the disciplinary chamber, Chabela hesitated.
Never having been in this part of the palace, she did
not know which way to go. She was, however, fiercely
determined to avoid recapture at any cost.

Peering down the empty, stone-lined corridor, she
decided that she must be in the crypts rumored to lie
beneath the palace of the Amazon queen. These chambers, she understood, were jealously guarded against
intruders; she might well, therefore, run into a guard
at any moment. Choosing a corridor that seemed to
slope upward, she set out at a rapid pace.

The silence was complete, save for the distant drip
of water and occasionally the scuttle of tiny claws. At
long intervals, a torch of oil-soaked wood, set in a
bracket of greened bronze, illumined the corridor with
a fitful yellow light. But so far apart were these torches
that between them the darkness thickened almost to
utter blackness. In these dark stretches, Chabela
glimpsed a pair of eyes like ruby chips at ground level,
as scurrying rodents paused to stare at her.

In the sinister silence, the naked girl glided like a
white phantom through the gloom, her nerves stretched
taut with terror. She felt the pressure of unseen eyes —
or was it only her own nerves?

The corridor curved and angled and forked. Forced
to guess which way to take, Chabela soon realized that
she was lost and wandering at random. She could no
doubt retrace her steps, but that would only bring her
back into Nzinga's dreaded clutches. There was nothing
to do but keep on, praying to Mitra to lead her back
into the open air.

After more wanderings, Chabela saw that she had
reached the dungeon area. On either hand stood copper-
barred cell doors. In the gloom of the cells behind lay

half-seen captive things, some of which moaned or sobbed but most of which were silent.

The girl peered into the first few cells she passed, but the sights she glimpsed were so repulsive that thereafter she averted her eyes and kept them on the path before her. Some of the prisoners were emaciated to skeletons, as by years of starvation. Some stared blankly from mad eyes out of matted hair. Bodies were scabrous with sores and coated with filth. Some had died, and the scavenger rats had stripped the scrawny flesh from their bones, leaving only skeletons.

Turning a curve in the corridor, Chabela was astonished to come upon a cell containing Conan the Cimmerian.

His massive body sprawled on thick straw in one of the cells. She stopped dead, wondering if she had gone mad or if it was truly the burly buccaneer who lay therein.

It was indeed the Cimmerian. At first she thought him dead, he lay so still. Then, as her eyes became accustomed to the gloom of the cell, she observed the rise and fall of his mighty chest. He was evidently unconscious.

Hesitantly she called his name, but this elicited nothing but a snore from the recumbent barbarian. She tested the cell door; it was securely locked.

Chabela lingered, wondering what to do. At any moment, Nzinga's guards might come clanking around the curve of the corridor and find her. The wise course would be to press on – yet she could not abandon to his fate the redoubtable buccaneer who had rescued her from the Nameless Isle.

Again she called his name in a desperate whisper. Then her eyes lighted upon an earthenware jug, standing against the wall. A probing finger discovered that it contained cold water. It must be the water that was doled out daily to the wretches in the cells.

Chabela hoisted the pot in her arms and brought it to Conan's cell. Luckily, the unconscious Cimmerian had been flung into the cell in such a way that his upturned face lay near the bars.

The Zingaran girl therefore was able to pour the contents of the jug through the bars and on the sleeping

119

Cimmerian's face. Coughing, sputtering, and growling, Conan came back to a groggy awareness. With a groan, he heaved himself up to a sitting posture glaring blearily about.

'What in Ymir's frozen hells—' he grumbled. Then his dull gaze fastened itself on the pale, frightened face of the Naked Zingaran princess, and he came fully awake.

'You? What in Crom's name is happening, girl?' he growled. Staring about with a puzzled expression, he continued: 'Where in the eleven scarlet hells *are* we? What's been going on? My skull feels as if all the demons of the Pit had been kicking it around . . .'

In low, terse words, the girl described her recent misadventures. Conan's lionlike gaze narrowed as he reflectively rubbed a stubbled jaw.

'So Nzinga drugged me, did she? I might have expected it, curse her jealous black heart! She didn't want me awake lest I interfere with the punishment she planned for you. She must have decided that my quarters in the harem were not secure enough and bade her servants bear me down here for safekeeping.' He fingered the straw on which he had lain and gave a low rumble of laughter. 'This straw is luxury by her ideas. It looks as if she meant to keep me on as her fancy man, to service her after she'd gotten rid of you.'

'What can we do, Captain Conan?' asked Chabela, almost in a whimper. The ordeal had nearly exhausted her considerable store of courage.

'Do? Conan grunted and spat. 'Make a break for it! Stand clear of the door.'

'What do you? I have no key—'

'To hell with keys!' he snarled, setting his huge hands on one of the bars. 'These bars are of soft copper and have been here for ages. Corrosion has bitten into them; and, if it has gone far enough, I need no keys. Stand back, now!'

Setting one foot against a bar, Conan bent his shoulders and heaved on the bar he grasped, which was green with verdigris. All of the coiled, terrific strength of his back, shoulders, and brawny arms went into one titanic effort. His face darkened; his breath came hoarsely. Drops of sweat on his broad forehead glistened in the torchlight. His thews stood out in bronze relief, like woven metal cables.

Chabela drew in her breath and bit her lip.

With a faint scream, the bar pulled out of the lower socket in the door frame; the metal bent and yielded. Then, with a thunderous crack, the bar broke. The report was like the snapping of a great whip.

Conan dropped the bar with a muffled clang on the straw. He sagged against the wall, drinking in great lungsful of air. Then he squeezed through the gap in the bars, turning sideways to do so, and stood in the corridor.

Chabela stared wide-eyed. 'Never have I seen such strength!' she breathed.

Conan massaged his arms. 'I shouldn't care to have to try that every day,' he said with a grin. Then, peering along the corridor: 'Which way? How do we get out of here? And who's been whipping you? Nzinga?'

She nodded and in quick, terse words outlined the events that had taken place since the incident in the dining chamber. Conan growled, his eyes kindling.

'A strange tale,' he said, 'and the strangest part of it is this magical apparition of a Stygian sorcerer – for such I take him to be. I have met his kind in my wanderings before. But I wonder who he is, who came to seize the Crown? You're sure it was not that skull-faced dog Menkara? He was skulking at Zarono's heels in Kordava.'

Chabela shook her head, so that her black, glossy curls tossed. 'Nay. I saw Menkara oft on the *Wastrel* and should know him at once. He is a gaunt, sad-looking fellow of medium size, who speaks in a dull, listless voice as if the world utterly wearied him. This man, albeit methinks of the same race, was very different: much taller, powerful, not unhandsome, with an air of vitality and command.'

Only half heeding, Conan sent his glance roving the corridor. He intuitively felt the need for action. If they were ever to escape from the city of warrior women, it must be now, while Queen Nzinga lay unconscious. How much longer she would slumber under the power of the Stygian's green ray, he had no way of knowing.

Conan led the way off down the winding corridor. He

121

paused to pull from its bracket a heavy torch. He hefted it with an appreciative grunt. At least, he had something to defend himself with. The torch was a club of a dense, glossy wood, the charred upper end of which had been wrapped round and round in bands of coarsely woven cloth, which in turn had been soaked in some viscous oil. The oil sent up a smoky, wavering yellow flame. One of Chabela's tasks as a slave had been to replace these torches as they burnt out around the palace and to rewrap and rekindle those that had become exhausted.

An unexpected turn in the corridor brought Conan and the princess face to face with a squad of woman soldiers. They were big, strapping females, with strong arms, flat pendulous breasts, and broad-cheeked, slit-eyed faces. They wore crude breastplates of leather, to which squares of bronze were tied by thongs, and kilts of leathern straps similarly studded. They carried throwing-spears and short, bronze-bladed swords.

'Seize them!' yelled a harsh voice, and Conan looked beyond the grim rank of Amazons to see Nzinga herself. The queen's handsome black face was distorted with fury. He grinned mirthlessly; there was no way out of this but to fight.

Conan was a barbarian from Cimmeria, and to him many of the ways of the South seemed soft, effeminate, and corrupt. But he was not without a certain rude chivalry of his own, and he did not like the idea of fighting and perhaps slaying women. Still, when it was a question of either fighting or being recaptured, he fought.

He did not await attack but sprang among the Amazons with one great bound, striking right and left with the blazing torch. In a trice he had felled two of the hulking woman warriors, whom he laid out of action with cracked skulls. A snarling Amazon lunged at him with a short sword; he shoved the torch into her face. She fell back with a scream, beating at her wooly hair as it blazed up. An assegai was thrust at his midriff; he knocked it out of its wielder's hand and sent it clanging against the wall. Moving with the speed of a pouncing

122

panther, he swung the torch up for another blow – and froze.

Nzinga had circled around the melee of struggling warriors. Now she stood with one brawny arm around the naked Zingaran princess. Her free hand held a needle-pointed dagger against Chabela's throat.

'Throw down that torch, white dog, or your bitch will choke on her own blood!' the Amazon queen commanded in a cold, deadly voice.

Conan cursed luridly, but there was nothing else to do. The torch clattered to the flagstones.

The Amazons surrounded him. Thick cords of woven dried grass were wound around his wrists, back and forth. His arms were lashed to his sides with the same material. The metallurgy of the backward Amazon country was still not up to the manufacture of complex fetters and locks. The locks on the cell doors, Conan supposed, had been inherited from the original builders of the city.

'He is safe now, O Queen,' boomed a woman warrior. 'Why not put him to the sword at once?'

Nzinga looked over Conan's sweat-glistening torso appraisingly. 'Nay,' she said at last. 'I have another doom in mind for the traitor. He who spurns my love shall not be indifferent to my hatred. Put them both in the slave pen until dawn. Then take both and cast them to the *kulamtu* trees!'

It seemed to Conan that, at the mention of that unfamiliar name, even the hardened, burly Amazons flinched. But what could be so terrible about a mere tree?

Chapter 16

THE DEVOURING TREE

CONAN BLINKED, squinting against the slanting rays of the rising sun as it soared above the treetops of the distant jungle. He stared about him curiously.

The Amazons had dragged the Zingaran girl and himself into the central square of Gamburu. To one side rose the royal palace, with the two age-worn, cryptic statues flanking its gate. Conan lay in the broad, shallow pit in the center of the square, on the sandy surface that formed its floor. When he had glimpsed this feature on his first arrival in Gamburu, Conan had noted the resemblance of this depression to an area, like that which he had seen in his mercenary days in Argossean Messantia. But the Messantian area had included pit doors whereby gladiators or wild beasts could be loosed into the arena to work upon each other or their victims. This arena had no such portals.

Another odd thing was the clump of trees in the center of the sandy floor. These must be the kulamtu trees of which Queen Nzinga had spoken. He looked the nearest one over and found it unlike any tree he had ever seen, although it had some faint resemblance to a banana tree. The trunk had a spongy, fibrous look; but instead of tapering to a point, it ended at the top in a round, wet-looking orifice, like a mouth. Below this orifice grew a circle of huge leaves, each one as large as a man – long, broad, and thick, with their upper surfaces covered with hairlike projections a finger's breadth in length.

Amazons resplendent in leopard skins, nodding plumes, and jingling barbaric jewelry, were slowly filling the rising tiers of stone seats that ringed the arena. Among these were many notables known to Conan from their mutual attendance at Nzinga's feasts.

Surreptitiously, he tested his bonds. Ropes of muscle stood out boldly along his bronzed arms; his brows contorted with effort. But the woven ropes resisted his best efforts – yielding a little but retaining their implacable grip on his arms and legs, which were also bound together by a rope around the ankles. How ironic, he thought, that he who had in his time broken chains of iron should now be defeated by cords of woven grass! Those who had bound his arms and legs, however, had known their business.

The benches were now nearly full. At a shout from Queen Nzinga, who sat amongst her grandees, the guards dragged Conan and Chabela close to the clump of strange-looking trees. Then they hastily retreated, leaving the two captives lying helplessly in the sand.

All around the pit, the Amazons kept up a rising spate of talk. Now they were pointing, jabbering, shoutin, laughing, and generally carrying on.

Chabela screamed. At the same time, Conan felt a touch on his foot and looked to see the cause. 'Crom!' he burst out.

One of the huge leaves of the kulamtu tree had reached down and was curling slowly around his ankle. Chabela screamed again, and Conan looked to see her limbs enfolded in the frond of another tree.

Conan set his jaw. This part of Kush was unfamiliar to him. But years before, when he had ravaged the Black Coast with Belit, he had heard tales of horrors of the inner jungles from her black crew. These rumors had included a story of a man-eating tree; but Conan had put this down to one more tall tale of superstitious barbarians.

Now he paled beneath his swarthy tan, for he understood the litter of dry, white human bones about the bases of these trees. The sticky fronds would curl slowly about his body, jerkily lift him up to that obscene-looking orifice, and pop him in. The devil-tree would swallow him alive. The acids secreted by the inner tissues would dissolve his flesh, and the tree would finally regurgitate his bare bones.

Three of the big fronds had curled about his body now, despite his thrashings and efforts to roll away. Slowly, they heaved him upright. Every one of the hair-like projections on the leaves stung like a hornet's sting where it touched him. Terror and revulsion lent new strength to his powerful muscles.

Then, beneath the shrill shouting from the benches, Conan heard a faint sound that lent new vigor to his thews. This sound was the snap of one of the grass cords as it parted. Then another one gave.

In a flash, Conan realized that the leaves, too, secreted a corrosive fluid, and that this fluid was dissolving and weakening the grass cords. He strained frantically, and more of the cords gave. An arm came free, and with his liberated hand he tore away a leaf that was starting to wrap itself about his head. He broke more cords, tore at the clinging, sticky leaves – and fell with a thump to the sand. His limbs, where the leaves had been in contact with them, were covered with itching red spots.

From the roar that exploded from the benches of the arena, Conan surmised that this had never happened before. Doubtless the Amazons had hitherto been prudent enough to feed their man-eating trees only victims weakened by torture or imprisonment. They had never offered to their vegetable executioners a man of unusual size and strength, in full possession of his powers. Ripping the last clinging leaf away, Conan grimly resolved to make the most of their error.

Chabela, now swathed like a mummy from head to foot in thick leaves, was halfway to the mouth of her tree when Conan got to her. He sprang up, caught the fronds that were lifting her, and clung. His added weight was too much for the leaves. They broke, some tearing in half and some pulling loose from the trunk altogether. Conan fell sprawling on the hot sands, holding the girl in his arms. Quickly he stripped away the leaves that enshrouded her, which, as he tore at them, slowly writhed as if in pain. Like his own skin, hers was red-dotted where the leaves had caressed it. Then he tugged at the grass cords that bound her. These, like his own, had been largely eaten through, so that it took no great effort to break them and set the girl free.

The Amazons were now in an uproar. A number of guardswomen had leaped down into the arena and were thudding toward him, the sun flashing on the bronze of their harness and weapons. Conan ripped away the last leaf from Chabela's face, so that she could breathe, and sprang to meet these human adversaries.

They did not, as he expected, pour down upon him

with spear and sword and club. Instead, they halted a few yards away, brandishing their weapons and yelling threats and epithets. Then he realized that it was not merely Conan, standing before them bare-handed and naked but for a lioncloth, of whom they were wary, but the trees behind him. Their hesitancy might stem from simple fear of the loathsome man-eating plants, or the trees might be regarded as gods. Whatever the reason, their hesitancy gave him an idea.

Turning, he set his shoulder against the tree that had attempted to make a morsel of him. This tree was now writhing and flapping its broken fonds as if in pain, making no more effort to seize Conan. The trunk had a flimsy, fibrous look and perhaps was no stronger than the stem of a plantain tree, which it resembled.

Conan hurled his weight against the trunk and felt it give slightly, with a ripping sound. Another heave, and the trunk tore out of the ground, the loose-packed sand of which gave little purchase to the network of white tendrils that served the cannibal tree as roots.

A howl of unholy outrage roared from the stands as Conan broke down the tree. He hefted it under his arm like a battering ram. It was about ten feet long from roots to mouth, a foot or so thick, and surprisingly light for so bulky an object.

Conan charged the women warriors, using the tree as a ram. They broke and fled squealing from his advance. He laughed exultantly. The Amazons evidently had a horror of their own sacred tree and sought to escape its proximity. He spun about, knocking down two of the guards with a swing of the trunk. The others fled back to the stands.

Now javelins began to fall about him in a deadly rain. One went *thunk* into the trunk a hand's breadth from his arm. Several angular throwing-knives whirled past his head like boomerangs.

'Chabela!' he roared. 'Grab one of those spears and follow me!'

The pair of them ran to the stands, Conan in the lead. A knot of Amazons in front of him broke and scattered as he swung the upper end of the tree among them, spattering drops of corrosive sap. The two climbed nimbly up the benches to the level of the square and loped for the street leading to the West Gate.

When he emerged from the pit, Conan fully expected to see half the female army of Gamburu assembled to attack him. Instead, a strangely different vista met his eyes as he clambered out of the arena. Fire arrows flickered through the air; nearby roofs blazed. A dozen corpses sprawled in puddles of gore, with shafts protruding from their bodies. A chorus of booming war cries rang through the air. The city of the Amazons was under attack.

A mass of black warriors, indisputably male, had poured out of the street to the West Gate. They formed disciplined ranks and advanced smartly, shooting sheets of arrows and cutting down the clusters of Amazons who charged their line.

Over the heads of the archers, Conan sighted his old comrade Juma and yelled his name. Juma saw him, grinned, and roared a command in the tongue of his own people. The ranks broke, and the archers rushed to surround and shelter Conan, who cast aside his tree, and the Zingaran girl. Then the force began to defile back out of the square the way they had come, fighting a cool rearguard action.

Conan laughed and clouted Juma on the shoulder. 'I wondered if you were coming,' he said. 'You got here just in time!'

Juma laughed and caught an Amazonian arrow on his long shield of tough rhinoceros hide. 'I don't know, Conan; you seemed to be doing all right.'

As they worked their way back to the West Gate, Juma explained that his men had finally tracked the slavers here to Gamburu. Then he had assembled a levy of his black warriors and marched on the Amazonian capital.

'I feared we should never find you alive,' he concluded. 'I ought to have realized that, being Conan, you'd be found in the midst of a fight as usual and taking on the whole Amazon city single-handed.'

As they reached the gate, Conan sighted the red-gold beard and blue eyes of Sigurd, who had been left there with a squad of armed sailors to keep the black army's line of retreat open. Conan and Sigurd shouted and waved but had no time for explanations.

Emerging from the gate, Conan smiled, happy to see the last of Queen Nzinga's city. The queen was a magnificent woman and had been a spectacular bedmate, but Conan was never one to be satisfied with the role of 'Mister Queen,' and he suspected that more than one former lover of the black queen had preceded him into the maws of the man-eating trees whenever the fickle and headstrong Nzinga had tired of their embraces.

'I see what you mean about training your archers in Turanian style,' he said to Juma. A rabble of Amazons rushed out of the gate in pursuit; but Juma's men deployed, closed ranks, and sent volleys of arrows into the throng until the survivors broke and fled back into their city.

Soon they reached the shelter of the trees. Then, while the force paused for breath, Conan and Sigurd greeted each other lustily. Sigurd cast an eye on Chabela and dropped to one knee.

'Princess!' he said in a scandalized voice. 'By Ishtar's teats and Moloch's fiery belly, you should ought to get some clothes on! What would your royal sire think? Here, take this!'

The Vanr stripped off his shirt and pressed it upon the girl, who put it on and rolled up the sleeves. Because of Sigurd's great size, the shirt was long enough to cover Chabela's well-rounded body.

'My thanks, Master Sigurd,' said she. 'You are right, of course; but I have been compelled to go naked among naked folk for so long that I had become used to it.'

'Whither now, Conan?' said Sigurd. 'I know not about you, but I've had enough of this sweltering jungle land. If the mosquitoes and leeches don't eat you alive, the lions are happy to finish what's left.'

'Back to Kulalo,' said Conan, 'and then aboard the *Wastrel* without delay. If the men left behind have sailed off and left us, I'll skin them alive.'

'Surely you will share our victory feast!' protested Juma. 'Now that my warriors have bested the Amazons of Gamburu, my empire is certain to dominate all this land. My men are eager to drink themselves into a stupor on good banana wine . . .'

Conan shook his head. 'I thank you, but I fear we cannot spare the time, old friend. We have our work cut out for us back in Zingara. There's some plot against the Princess Chabela's sire, King Ferdrugo, and we must get her home at once. It seems that half the magicians of Stygia are joined in the scheme, so the victory feast will have to wait. Our victory, you see, has yet to be won.'

Chapter 17

THE WRECK OF THE WASTREL

THE TRIP through the jungles from Gamburu to King Juma's capital of Kulalo, and thence to the mouth of the Zikamba, where they had left the *Wastrel*, consumed a number of days. Chabela was too exhausted to make the journey on foot, so Juma's blacks quickly built a rude litter of bamboo and rough cloth, in which the princess made the trip in relative comfort.

As for Conan, a few hours of rest, half a goatskin of strong wine, and a huge slab of roast meat rendered him fit again. Not for the first time, the magnificent animal vitality of Conan's barbarian heritage had shown him superior to the weaker, softer men of the countries through which he wandered and adventured. He took no special pride in this physical preeminence, reasoning that it was the doing of his forebears or of the gods and hence no cause for self-conceit.

It was sundown when they reached the palmy fringes of the Zikamba. The moon was rising like a copper shield by the time they came to the mouth of the river. There the stream spread out in an estuary. The sluggish flood mingled its fresh water, dark with sediment, with the booming sea. And there, a shocking sight awaited them.

Sigurd gasped, recovered, and gave voice to a sulphurous sequence of oaths. Conan said nothing, but the impassive bronze mask of his face darkened with fury.

For the *Wastrel* lay half sunk in the shallows, her decks awash. Her masts were mere charred stumps, for fire had swept her deck. From these facts and the dozen burial mounds of heaped earth that stood along the edge of the jungle, the Cimmerian grimly surmised that there had been a battle and that the *Wastrel* had lost.

The sound of the approach of Juma's party roused alert sentries. There were cries of warning and the thud of footsteps. Torches flared and flashed on naked cutlasses in the hands of a band of burly seamen. Conan thrust his companions aside and strode forward.

They were in sorry condition. Most were wrapped in dirty bandages, and some limped on sticks and crutches. The mate, Zeltran, bustled up. His right arm was swathed in bandages; he carried his saber in his left.

'Captain!' he yelled. 'Is it you? Sink me, but we never thought to see you again. The jungles seemed to have swallowed you up!'

'I live, Zeltran,' said Conan. 'But what's befallen here? There has been trouble, I see, but from whom?'

Zeltran shook his head sorrowfully. The rotund little mate had lost weight. 'That dog Zarono!' he snarled. 'Three days ago, his *Petrel* took us by surprise—'

'Surprise?' roared Conan. 'How could that happen? Had you no lookouts?'

Zeltran cursed. 'Lookouts a-plenty, my Captain, but all the lookouts in the world could not have seen the *Petrel*. A dense fog crept in upon us – such a fog as these eyes have never seen. One could see no further than one can see through a granite cliff—'

'Aye, Captain, 'tis true!' said a seaman. ''Twas witch-craft, Captain Conan – black sorcery, fry my guts if it wasn't!'

'And under cover of this mysterious fog bank, the *Petrel* sailed in and swept your decks, is that it?' Conan growled.

Zeltran said: 'Aye, sir; that be just how it happened. First thing we knew was the crunch of Zarono's side against ours, and then his men poured over the rail and had at us. We fought, the gods know – you can see our wounds – but they had the upper hand in numbers and surprise. In the end, they drove us over our shoreward rail and into the water. I tried to cover my lads' retreat—'

'Aye, Captain,' said another seaman. 'Ye should have seen him – 'twould have made you proud – whacking away with his cutlass like three men.'

'—but then something hit me over the head. When I came to, I was tied to the mast, with Zarono's dogs standing around and grinning. Then comes black Zarono himself, all very elegant in his lace ruffles, with that snaky priest Menkara behind him.

132

' "Oho, my fine lad," says Zarono, "and where's your master, the barbarian lout Conan?"

' "Gone ashore, sir," I says.

'Zarono hits me a clip across the mouth. "I can see that fool," he says, "but where ashore?"

' "I know not, sir," I says, not seeing that it would do any good to enrage the man. "He is friends with some gang of black warriors that live hereabouts, and he has gone off to visit them."

' "And where's that Zingaran lass he had with him?" says Zarono.

' "Gone with him, as far as I know," I says.

' "But which way, man? Which way, and how far?" says Zarono.

'I pretended a great ignorance of King Juma's whereabouts, even when they tickled my right arm with hot coals. I will show you the blisters, my Captain, when they heal up a little more. Then Zarono and the Stygian priest went aside and consulted in low tones. The priest set up his magical apparatus on the quarterdeck, and mumbled and grumbled for a long time, while strange lights flickered about him. At last he says to Zarono: "I see her being borne in a litter along a jungle trail in the midst of a powerful host of black warriors. More I cannot tell you."

'That made Zarono fair furious, I can tell you. He hit me in the face a few times, just to take out his anger. "How in the names of all the gods," says he, "am I supposed to comb all the vast jungles of Kush to find the wench, and then snatch her out from an army of hundreds of fierce barbarians? As well ask me to jump over the moon!"

'After more palaver, Zarono and Menkara decided to destroy the *Wastrel* and depart at once for Kordava. They planned to go by way of Stygia to gather up their confederate, who if I heard aright is called Thoth-Amon.'

'Thoth-Amon?' said Conan. 'I've crossed his trail before. A bad enemy to have, from all I hear. But go on. Those two dogs seem to have been pretty free with their talk in front of you.'

'Ah, but my Captain, they did not expect me to live to tell tales! Zarono gave his orders. One crew went alongside in their longboat and chopped a hole in the hull at the waterline. Another party piled fuel around the masts and set it alight.'

'And you were tied to one of these masts?'

'Exactly, sir. The mainmast, in fact. Naturally, I did not take kindly to the idea of being burnt alive; so, while Zarono's people scrambled back aboard the *Petrel* and shoved off – not wishing to burn their own ship as well – I prayed to Mitra and Ishtar and Asura and every other god I ever heard of to get me out of this fix. And whether or not my prayers were heard, no sooner had the *Petrel* vanished in the fog than it began to rain.

'Meanwhile, the *Wastrel* settled from the hole in her bottom until she rested on the ground as you see her now. And I wriggled and struggled and finally got my arms out of the ropes, for the Petrels had not done a very seamanlike job of tying me up. And when I was free, I kicked most of the combustibles overboard, and the rain put out the rest of the fire – although not before the masts and rigging had been consumed. And here we are.'

Conan grunted. 'He'd have been cleverer not to have tried both to sink and to burn the ship. One or the other, but both at once cancel each other out.' He clapped Zeltran on the shoulder, bringing a yelp of pain from the mate as his sore arm was jostled. 'I believe you and the boys did all you could. But now we must plan our next step, which is to make the *Wastrel* seaworthy again as quickly as may be.'

Zeltran pulled a doleful face. 'Alas, my Captain, I see not how to do that in less than several months' time. We have no shipyard, nor can we whistle up a swarm of skilled shipwrights out of this jungle.'

Juma had stalked silently forward. 'My men will aid you in repairing your ship,' he said. 'Many strong hands make a task easy.'

'Perhaps, and I thank you,' said Conan thoughtfully. 'But what do your warriors know of repairing ships?'

'Naught; we are no seagoing folk. But we are many and strong, and we have among us good craftsmen in wood. If your men will lead them and show them what is to be done, they will work like giants until the task be finished.'

'Good!' said Conan. He raised his voice to his dispirited crew. 'Shipmates, we have lost a battle, but we have not yet lost the war! Black Zarono, who overcame you by treacherous sorcery, now sails the sea bound for Zingara, where he hopes to topple our friend and patron, old King Ferdrugo. King Juma's people will help us to put our ship to rights. Then ho for the main, to get revenge upon the scoundrel and save our king from his plots! What say you?'

'We lost a lot of good men,' said the boatswain, nodding toward the row of graves.

'Aye, but we have Sigurd's Argosseans! If ye'll all pull together as one crew, with no more folly of Barachan against buccaneer, we can do it. So what say ye? Let me hear you, loud and clear!'

The sailors roared their approval, and their cutlasses flashed in the moonlight.

Never had Conan seen men work so hard. They belayed cables to the stumps of the burnt masts and dragged the ship upright. They dove into the water-filled hold to fetch out tools. They felled trees, cut them into boards, and patched the hole in the *Wastrel*'s side. They pumped out the water until the ship once again floated free on her anchor cables.

They felled more trees and shaved them down to size to take the place of the burnt masts and spars. While the women of Juma's capital stitched new canvas, the men gathered resinous firewood, piled it in ricks, lighted it, and collected the tar that ran out from under the piles. The work went on day and night, while boys from Juma's people held torches aloft for illumination.

Then came the day of departure. The buccaneers were reeling with fatigue or drunk on banana wine or both; but the *Wastrel* would be ready to catch the dawn breeze.

Throughout the black night, Juma's people filed in a long line through the Kushite jungle to the shore, bearing provisions: casks of water, kegs of tough millet cakes, bales of fresh fruit, sides of smoked pork, barrels of yams and other vegetables; provisions enough to feed the buccaneers on a journey to the other side of the world.

As dawn paled the skies to the east, Conan bade farewell to Juma. Once they had fought side by side in the legions of King Yildiz of Turan; again, they had dared the snows of the trackless Talakmas, the yelling horde of slant-eyed little warriors in fantastic armor of lacquered leather, and the walking stone idol in the unknown valley of Meru. Now, for the last time, they had fought side by side in the sweltering Kushite jungles.

Silently, grinning but blinking back tears, they clenched each other's hands in a fierce grip. They said nothing, for both somehow guessed that they would not meet again in this incarnation.

The *Wastrel* hoisted sail. Canvas boomed as it filled and tautened in the offshore breeze. Black warriors with their women and naked children lined the shore to wave farewell. And the *Wastrel* rode out into deep water and set course for Zingara.

Chapter 18

A KINGDOM IN THE BALANCE

At sundown, Conan brought the *Wastrel* into the harbor of Kordava. A heavy overcast blotted out the stars as the day died.

Few eyes noted the lean carack as she glided silently into the great curve of the harbor and nosed gently into a little-used moorage at the far end of the quays. Conan thought it wise to enter the city as unobtrusively as possible, since he did not know whether Duke Villagro had already seized the reins of power, nor how long Zarono and Thoth-Amon had been in the city. That they had preceded him, he was certain when Zeltran touched his arm and pointed:

'Zarono's *Petrel*!' hissed the mate. 'My Captain, it strikes me that, since nobody seems to be about, we could rush it and burn it—'

Conan grinned in the gloom. 'Control yourself, my little fighting cock,' he growled. 'Who's being rash now? We play for bigger stakes. Our friends are probably not there, but up in Ferdrugo's castle, spinning their webs to entrap the old fellow.'

The princess tugged at Conan's arm impatiently. 'Let us hasten to the palace, Captain Conan! Your men can follow later. We must warn my father at once of the schemes against him, ere those traitors, Villagro and Zarono, can—'

'Easy all,' said Conan with a grin. 'A bit less hasty, girl! I've learned long since not to walk into a trap if I can avoid it. The rebel duke and this sorcerer Thoth-Amon may have already seized power, and to go straight to the palace were to play fly to their spider. Nay, I have another goal in mind—'

'What goal?' the girl demanded.

He smiled grimly. 'First we shall visit the one place in Kordava where I shall be safe; the Nine Drawn Swords.'

'The Nine Drawn Swords?' she repeated.

'Not the sort of place that ladies of your quality would

patronize, but 'twill do for our purposes. Trust me, lass! Zeltran, I will take ten men. Fetch boat cloaks and lanterns, and see that all are well armed beneath their cloaks.'

The streets were as silent as those of a necropolis. Sigurd, superstitious like all seamen, shivered as he stamped through puddles by Conan's side, while his hand fondled the hilt of his cutlass under his black cloak.

'Surely they are all dead or under a curse,' he grumbled, peering about with wary eyes. Conan bade him hold his tongue for fear of arousing the watch.

Thus, none save the cats of Kordava saw the party of seamen that, muffled in black boat cloaks with their faces hidden, slunk silently through the alleys to the door of the Nine Drawn Swords. As they filed in, old Sabral came puffing up to the door, wiping his hands on his apron.

' 'Tis sorry I am, but we are closed for the night,' he said. 'The government has told all taverns to shut up shop at sundown this night. So I'll have to ask you to – oh!'

Conan had doffed his hat, thrown back his cloak, and thrust the grim bronze mask of his face close to that of the taverner. 'What's that, my friend?' he murmured.

'Ah, had I but known you at first . . . But of course the Nine Drawn Swords be always open to Captain Conan, laws or no laws. Come in, lads, come in. 'Twill take a bit of time to light the fires and break out the drinkables, but what ye want ye shall have.'

'Why should the government ask you to close early tonight?' asked Conan, settling himself at ease where he could watch the door.

The fat innkeeper shrugged. 'Mitra only knows, Captain! A royal decree from the palace, came out yestereve . . . These be strange times, strange times indeed. First Captain Zarono comes ashore, the gods know whence, with a squad of dusky Stygians amongst his crew, and walks right into King Ferdrugo's palace as if he owned the place. Not a word said to him, as if he'd laid the king's people under a spell. And then all these new decrees: the city gates shut at sundown, and so forth. Duke Villagro made provost marshal, and the city placed

138

under martial law. Passing strange, captain; passing strange it be. And no good will come of it, you mark my words!'

'That's curious,' said Sigurd.

'What's curious?' asked Conan.

'Well, Dagda's eye and Orvandel's toe! Your friend Sabral says the city's locked up as tight as a drum, but we sailed into the harbor without a hail. Wouldn't you think Villagro would have set his cutthroats to guard the harbor?'

'They think the *Wastrel*'s still lying on her side at the mouth of the Zikamba,' said Conan.

'Ah, yes!' rejoined Sigurd. 'I was forgetting. Zarono would never guess that, with the help of Juma's folk, we should get the ship repaired so swiftly.'

Conan nodded. 'Aye, redbeard. If all goes well now, King Ferdrugo may owe his throne to a black warrior he never heard of and will never see!'

'I've never thought much of the blacks before,' said Sigurd. 'They always seemed to me a pack of superstitious, childish savages. But your friend Juma opened my eyes. He's a real leader, even as you yourself are. Aye, there's heroes and there's scuts in every folk and nation.'

But there was little time for idle talk. Conan queried Sabral, who volubly explained many things that the buccaneer guessed or feared might be taking place. Villagro had not yet seized the throne, but the event might be only hours away. Loyal garrisons had been sent to the borders on various pretexts. Officers noted for loyalty to the dynasty had been sent abroad, or dismissed, or arrested and jailed on trumped-up charges. Since sundown of this day, the palace had been sealed off from the rest of the city. Key guard posts were held by Villagro's adherents. A ceremony of some kind was to take place in the palace; but just what, Sabral could not even guess.

'Abdication, is my guess,' rumbled Conan, pacing the floor of the inn like a caged lion. 'We must get into the palace. But how? Villagro and Zarono have it sealed up. This Thoth-Amon must have Ferdrugo firmly under his thumb. But if we can confront the king with his daughter, the shock might break the spell . . . Then we can have at the traitors. Where's that cursed Ninus? He should have been here half an hour gone . . .'

Sigurd wrinkled his brow. Conan had asked Sabral about the health of his little priestly friend. The Zingaran innkeeper had replied that the ex-thief had recovered and returned to the sanctuary of his temple. Thereupon, Conan had dispatched a sailor to fetch the man to the Nine Drawn Swords.

'Who is this Ninus?' queried Sigurd.

Conan shrugged impatiently. 'I knew him years ago when he and I were thieves in Zamora. He returned to his native Zingara when even the scarlet city of Zamora became too hot for him. Here he fell in with a silver-tongued missionary of the Mitraist cult, who persuaded him that priests live on the fat of the land by playing on the fears and superstitions of honest burghers and bored housewives. Being one who always knew on which side his bread was buttered, he promptly got religious and became a priest of Mitra. But if there be anyone in Kordava who will know a secret entrance to Ferdrugo's palace, it will be he! He was the smartest thief I ever knew – even more so than Taurus of Nemedia, whom men called the prince of thieves. He could find doors no one else—'

A solemn gong note struck Conan's alert ears. Chabela stiffened and sank her nails into the flesh of Conan's arm.

'The bells in the tower of all the gods!' she gasped. 'Oh, Conan, we are too late!'

He bent a sharp gaze on her pale face. 'What mean you, girl? Quickly, now!'

'The bells – they announce that the king holds audience! We are too late – it has already begun . . .'

Conan and Sigurd exchanged a quick look and thrust open a window to look up at the palace on the hill.

Lights flickered and moved to and fro. Chabela had spoken truly; the ceremony had begun.

Chapter 19

KING THOTH-AMON

THE SCENE in the throne room of King Ferdrugo was one of tense drama. Fitful lightning flared in stormy skies without, and intermittent flashes of blue-tinged gray light flickered in the tall, pointed windows of diamond-paned glass.

The hall was huge and lofty. Circular walls and a ring of mighty columns of ponderous granite, faced with curved slabs of smooth marble, supported the enormous dome far above. This dome was the greatest architectural wonder of Ferdrugo's kingdom.

Huge candles, as thick as a warrior's biceps, shed a rich, wavering glow from mighty sconces of wrought gold. Torchlight and lamplight and lightning flashes were reflected from the mirrorlike polish of the shields and plume-crested helms of the guards stationed about the circumference of the hall.

There were many more guards present than was usual on such occasions. This in itself was a cause for uncertainty and suspicion on the part of the score of nobles and officials whom the king's heralds had summoned. The command had gone out in haste and in secret to be presented during the reading of a proclamation from the throne.

The other cause for concern was the livery of these guards. While some wore the uniforms of the Throne Legion – the king's private bodyguard – far more displayed the colors of Villagro, duke of Kordava.

In the center of the hall, on a raised dais of glistening, green, black-veined malachite, rested the ancient rose-marble throne of the Ramiran Dynasty. Therein was seated Ferdrugo III.

The assembled dignitaries had seen but little of their monarch in recent months. They watched the old man speculatively, for he had aged greatly during this time. His flesh seemed withered; his limbs, shrunken. His cheeks had fallen in, so that his cheekbones stood out in bold relief. Candlelight, falling from the sconces above, cast deep wells of black shadow beneath the prominent cheekbones, while the old man's eyes were lost in the dark shadows beneath his prominent eyebrow ridges and bushy white eyebrows. The lighting, together with his gaunt, frail aspect, lent the old monarch a ghastly semblance of a skeleton.

On his head, seeming too heavy for his thin, wattled neck to support, rested the ancient crown of the hero-king Ramiro, the founder of the dynasty. It was a plain ellipse of gold, with a castellated upper rim formed by simple, square projections, like the merlons and embrasures of the tower of a castle.

With waxen, transparent hands, the king clasped a large sheet of parchment, to which were affixed a number of seals. In a weak, uncertain voice, King Ferdrugo read from this sheet. The long formal preamble, the endless list of titles, the legalistic jargon all combined to feed the nervous speculation in the minds of the audience. None but felt the stirring of a premonition of dire events.

On the floor before the dais, directly in front of the throne, stood two men. One was the duke of Kordava. In the absence of Prince Tovarro, the king's younger brother, Villagro was, after the king himself, the ranking peer of the realm. The expression on his lean, hungry features might have been described as complacent expectancy combined with nervous apprehension.

Beside Villagro stood another figure, a stranger to the rest of those present. A Stygian he seemed, from his shaven head, hawklike features, dusky skin, and tall, broad-shouldered build. He was, however, heavily robed, so that nothing of him but his head could be seen.

On his shaven skull rested a curious headpiece: a crown made in the likeness of a golden serpent, coiled round the wearer's head and crusted with thousands of glittering white gems. Some of the notables had nudged each other and murmured at the sight, when the stranger had thrown back the hood of his robe, revealing this extraordinary headgear. If, they whispered, the gems were in truth cut diamonds – the making of which was virtually unknown in the Hyborian Age – the value of the crown must be beyond calculation. Whenever the stranger moved slightly, the gems sent out a thousand rays of all the colors of the rainbow, reflected from the light sources overhead and around the circuit of the hall.

The dark-faced man bore a look of intense concentration. Such was his inner absorption that he seemed hardly aware of those around him. It was as if all his energies were focused upon one single objective.

Among the retinue of Duke Villagro could be seen the sinister features of Zarono the buccaneer and, also, a hooded figure that some recognized as that of the Setite priest, Menkara, whom they knew vaguely as one of Villagro's hangers-on.

Ferdrugo feebly droned on, but now he neared the end of the document. Then the audience froze in amazement as the import of the words reached their astounded ears:

'. . . and thus, by these presents, We, Ferdrugo of Zingara, renounce the throne in favor of Our daughter and heiress, the Princess Royal Chabela, and wed her in absentia to her betrothed and your next king, the high prince Thoth-Amon of Stygia! Long live queen and king! Long live Chabela and Thoth-Amon, thus created queen and king of the ancient and imperishable kingdom of Zingara!'

All over the chamber, jaws sagged and eyes widened in astonishment. No visage showed greater shock than that of Duke Villagro of Kordava. He goggled at old King Ferdrugo; his sallow features paled to a leaden hue. His thin, rouged lips writhed back in a voiceless snarl, exposing yellowed teeth.

Villagro turned as if to speak to the tall, silent figure beside him. The impassive Stygian gave him a quiet smile, brushed aside his hand, and ascended the steps to the top of the dais as if to receive the plaudits of the throng. But there were no plaudits – only a rising buzz of astonishment and indignation.

Over the rising hum of voices rose the quavering tones of King Ferdrugo: 'Kneel, my son!'

The tall Stygian halted in front of the Zingaran king and dropped to one knee. He raised both hands, lifted the Cobra Crown from his head, and gently laid it on the green-and-black stone of the dais beside him.

Ferdrugo stepped forward and took from his own head the plain ancient crown of the hero-king Ramiro. He turned it about and, with quivering hands, lowered it gently down upon Thoth-Amon's shaven skull.

His face sick with the full realization of his ally's treachery, Villagro snatched at the ornamental dagger he wore at his girdle. Perhaps he meant to throw caution to the winds and drive the steel into the back of the great magician as he knelt. But then he released the dagger as his staring eyes focused with maniacal intensity upon the Cobra Crown, where it rested beside the kneeling Thoth-Amon. He knew, or thought he knew, something of its powers. In reporting to him, Zarono had explained:

'From what Menkara told me and from what Thoth-Amon let slip on the voyage hither, Your Grace, I believe that it works as follows. It amplifies and multiplies the power of the human mind to affect the minds of other beings. Thus Menkara, who is at best a middling wizard, can control the mind of one other person – in this case, our doddering king. Thoth-Amon, a magician of vastly greater powers, can govern several other minds at once. But he who wears the Crown, if he knows the proper methods, can by the Crown's power rule the minds of hundreds or even thousands of other beings. He can, for instance, drive a regiment of soldiers utterly recklessly until the last man of them be slain. He could dispatch a lion, a venomous serpent, or other deadly wild beast to seek out and destroy his enemy.

'None could stand against the wearer of the Cobra Crown. He could not be killed by ambush or assassination, for the Crown would convey to him the thoughts of those preparing the deed, and none could get within catapult shot of him without coming under his governance. Mortals like you and me, my lord, are ever plagued by the failure of our hirelings to carry out our commands – as when my sailors let the princess slip out of our grasp. But Thoth-Amon need fear no such blunders. When he issues a mental command, it will be carried out exactly, even at the cost of the henchman's life.'

And now, to seal Thoth-Amon's elevation to the throne, Ferdrugo was, with his own hands, placing the ancient crown of Zingara upon the Stygian's swarthy pate. To do so, however, it was necessary for Thoth-Amon to doff the Cobra Crown. In this act, Duke Villagro saw his opportunity.

Moving with a swiftness that belied his years, the duke hurled aside his velvet chaperon and bounded up the steps of the dais. Since Thoth-Amon was not wearing the Cobra Crown, the wizard had no warning of his former ally's action until Villagro snatched up the Cobra Crown and clapped it upon his own head.

As the duke started forward, he heard a muffled, guttural exclamation, which he recognized as the voice of nearby Menkara. With the Crown on his head, Villagro whirled, to see Menkara coming swiftly up behind him with a bared dagger in his bony fist.

As soon as the Cobra Crown settled upon his dyed and curled hair, Villagro was conscious of a host of sensations pouring through his mind. It seemed as if the unspoken thoughts of every person in the chamber rushed into his consciousness at once, in a buzzing, booming confusion. No magician, Villagro could not sort out these random thoughts.

As Menkara neared him, the duke in desperation focused his mind upon the priest, at whom he thrust out his fingers in what he conceived to be a wizardly gesture. With all his might, he concentrated on the mental picture of Menkara falling over backward, as if knocked down by a mighty blow of the fist.

And Menkara's rush did, in fact, slow and halt at the bottom step of the dais. As if struck, Menkara staggered back. His dagger tinkled to the pavement.

A leonine roar from behind him caused Villagro to whirl again. It came from Thoth-Amon, who had risen to his feet and turned about.

'Dog! For this you shall die!' shouted the Stygian, speaking Zingaran with a guttural accent.

'Die thyself!' replied Villagro, extending his fingers toward Thoth-Amon.

The mighty wizard was not to be easily overcome, even with the help of the Cobra Crown, because the wearer of that Crown was ignorant of and unpractised in its use. For a straining, quivering instant, the two men faced each other in a deadlocked contest of wills. The power of Villagro over others' minds with the

Crown roughly equaled the powers of Thoth-Amon, one of the greatest magicians of the age, without it. They strained and staggered, but neither yielded.

Below, the nobles and officials regarded the tableau with slack-jawed astonishment. There were many brave men among them, who would instantly have rallied to whichever side stood for the welfare of Zingara – but in these chaotic moments, who could tell which side that was? A king reduced to imbecility, a sinister foreign sorcerer, and a notoriously unscrupulous and conniving duke . . . who could say where lay the right?

Behind him, Villagro heard Menkara muttering a spell. He felt his own mental strength weakening. Before him Thoth-Amon seemed to grow in stature and might . . .

Then a sudden eruption of noise shook the room and brought all eyes about to stare at the source. A crowd of rough, ragged seamen boiled suddenly out of a portal on a balcony above the hall. At their head strode a bronzed giant with an unshorn mane of raven-black hair and burning eyes of volcanic blue under heavy black brows, with a huge cutlass clenched in one mighty fist.

Zarono uttered a shout of astonishment: 'Conan! By all the gods and devils – here!'

Seeing the burly barbarian appear so suddenly, the sallow-faced buccaneer paled. Then his lean, wolfish countenance grew grim, and his hard black eyes blazed with wrath. He slid his rapier from its sheath.

The interruption had also distracted Thoth-Amon, who turned his swarthy, golden-crowned head to stare. Had he worn the Cobra Crown, he would have known of the approach of Conan and his men before they appeared; but he had doffed the magical headpiece just before they came within its range.

After a glance at the intruders, Villagro returned his attention to Thoth-Amon. The Stygian, he knew, was by far the more dangerous foe. If he could, by the unpractised use of the Crown, vanquish Thoth-Amon, then Conan could easily be disposed of by the same means. But, if he turned his full attention on Conan, Thoth-Amon would wipe him out as easily as swatting an insect.

Conan strode to the head of the stair and windmilled his arms for attention.

'Ho, lords of Zingara!' he boomed. 'Vile treason and blackest magic have enmeshed your king in their toils!' One brawny arm shot out, pointing at the silent figure of the Stygian. 'No prince of Stygia he, but Hell's most stinking spawn! A sorcerer from the unholy depths of Stygia, come to steal the ancient throne of Zingara from its royal house. No blacker villain than Thoth-Amon has ever soiled the earth! Your king's wits have been stolen by some wizardly trick, so that he knows not what he says; he but parrots the thoughts that this would-be usurper puts into his mind!'

The assemblage wavered, some persuaded by Conan's words and some not. One fat nobleman cried: 'What madness is this? A wild-eyed rogue of a pirate, bursting into the palace during a sacred ceremony, waving his sword and shouting nonsense? Guards, arrest those rapscallions!'

A babble arose, over which Conan roared: 'Look at the king and see the truth of my words, you simpletons!'

Beside his throne, pale and shrunken, Ferdrugo wavered, plucking at his wispy white beard. 'What – what is happening here, my lords?' he quavered. His bewildered gaze swept from face to face. Then he noticed the document in his hand. 'What – what is this? Was I reading it?' he murmured. 'It makes no sense . . .'

It was obvious that King Ferdrugo did not recognize the proclamation that he had just read. Thoth-Amon, distracted by his contest with Villagro and Conan's intrusion, had let slip his mental control of Ferdrugo's will. Now his attention was forcibly brought back to the duke.

When Thoth-Amon had turned toward Conan, Villagro had hurled his will, amplified a thousand-fold by the Cobra Crown, at the looming form of the Stygian. Thoth-Amon staggered under the impact, nearly fell, and clutched the arm of the throne to steady himself. The Zingaran crown – which, being too small for him, rode unsteadily on his swarthy scalp – fell from his head and struck the stone of the dais with a clang.

Then he rallied. With the whites of his eyes showing

in a hypnotic glare, he in turn sent Villagro staggering with a mental blast.

'Give me the Cobra Crown, fool!' snarled Thoth-Amon.

'Never!' shrilled Villagro.

The duke felt an increase of the mental power opposing him. Behind him he felt, without seeing, the mind-force of Menkara added to that of Thoth-Amon. The priest of Set had rallied to the side of his master. Again Villagro felt himself weakening, his mental defenses crumbling.

Eyes swung back to where Conan and his buccaneers stood at the head of the stairs. The air was taut and crackling with suspense. It was one of those moments when the fate of nations is balanced on a knife blade – when a single word, a look, or a gesture can turn the tide of events and topple empires.

And then, in that momentary silence, the word was spoken. The figure of a young girl appeared at Conan's side. She was well-rounded, with sleek olive skin, dark flashing eyes, and hair of silken jet. Though her buxom young body was garbed in a rough sailor's costume, it came to the lords of Zingara that they had seen her before, in more sumptuous raiment.

'The princess!' gasped a baron.

'Eh? Chabela?' muttered the old king peering nervously about. All saw that it was truly she. But, before a babble of questions could arise, the girl spoke:

'Nobles of Zingara, Captain Conan speaks the truth! Yonder black-hearted Stygian schemer has caught my father in his magical toils. Conan rescued me from the sorcerer, and we have raced back to Kordava to forestall his usurpation! Strike him down, guards!'

The captain of the royal guard snapped an order to his troops and ripped out his sword with a rasp of steel against leather. He advanced at the head of his men.

Conan and nine sailors clattered down the stairs, blades flashing in the lamplight. Chabela remained at the head of the stairs with Ninus, the priest of Mitra. The little man dropped to his knees, and his high voice rose in a frantic prayer:

'O Lord Mitra, great prince of light!' he intoned. 'Stand by us in this hour against the dark power of Set!

148

In the divine name of Sraosha and by the unthinkable name, Zurvan, lord of infinite time, we pray and conjure thee! Strike with thine holy fire, that the Old Serpent be smitten and fall from his high place!'

Whether Thoth-Amon weakened from his titanic mental exertions, or whether Villagro's command of the Cobra Crown was becoming stronger with practice, or whether in sooth Mitra took a hand in the contest, Thoth-Amon seemed to pale, shrink, and weaken. He reeled back a step. Villagro opened his mouth for a shout of triumph.

Before the cry could come forth, Thoth-Amon played his last card. His long, brown forefinger shot out toward the duke of Kordava. A nimbus of jade-green radiance flickered into being about the finger and elongated into a beam of emerald light.

The beam struck the head of Duke Villagro and the diamond-crusted crown on that head, bathing it in a blinding emerald refulgence. Then the gold itself of the crown glowed red.

Villagro uttered a piercing scream. He reeled back, clutching at his head as if trying to tear off the crown. Black smoke curled up as his black-dyed hair blazed.

Then the room was bathed in a blinding blue light as lightning flashed just outside the chamber, filling the tall windows with a furious glare. One of the windows shattered with a tinkle of glass. A narrow sheet of rain poured slantingly in. To some in the chamber, half blinded by the glare and wholly deafened by the earth-shaking boom of thunder that instantly followed, it seemed that a tendril of lightning flicked through the broken window, to lash downward like a cosmic whip at the stricken duke of Kordava.

Villagro fell headlong, face down upon the pavement. The Cobra Crown came off and rolled across the marble, leaving Villagro's body with its hair burnt to a mere stubble and the skin around the skull, where the crown had touched it, seared to a black crisp.

So ended the ambitious dreams of Duke Villagro, who, dissatisfied with his ducal coronet, had yearned after kingly crowns and died of a surfeit of dreams.

Chapter 20

RED BLOOD AND COLD STEEL

FOR THREE heartbeats, this startling event held all the living persons in the chamber in a state of frozen shock. Thoth-Amon was the first to recover his wits.

'Menkara! Zarono!' he bellowed. 'Come here!' As the priest of Set and the buccaneer approached, the latter with his rapier in hand, the Stygian wizard said: 'Collect your men and Villagro's partisans! Strike hard and fast! If you do not, your heads will answer for it! With Conan on the king's side, you have no chance of making your peace with the old regime!'

'Where are your spells?' snarled Zarono. 'Why don't you sweep our foes away with a wave of your hand?'

'I will do what I can; but magic, too, has its limitations. To your arms!'

'You are right,' said Zarono, spinning on his heel. 'Men!' he shouted. 'The duke is dead, but the prince of Stygia lives! If our swords put him on the throne, we shall all be lords! To me!'

'All loyal Zingarans to me!' roared Conan. 'Strike for your king and your princess, and save Zingara from the rule of that devil from the Stygian hells!'

There was a general movement as the two parties sorted themselves out. Most of Villagro's partisans streamed toward Zarono, while most of the noblemen and officials clustered around Conan and his seamen. Some, uncertain which side to take or merely timid, slipped out of the hall.

It was soon to be seen that Zarono's party was the larger. While some palace guards joined Conan's faction, a larger number of men-at-arms, being Villagro's henchmen, sided with Zarono. All these soldiers were in half-armor, which gave them an advantage in battle.

'You are outnumbered!' shouted Thoth-Amon, from the dais. 'Surrender, and you will be allowed to flee with your lives!'

Conan responded with a loud, impolite suggestion to Thoth-Amon, as to what to do with his proposal.

'Out swords for Thoth-Amon, king of Zingara!' cried Zarono, rushing upon the nearest man of Conan's party.

Swords began to clash here and there. In a glittering rush, the two factions surged together. The rasp and chime of sword against sword resounded. The hall was alive with struggling, shouting, fighting men. Sword clanged against sword, helmet, cuirass, and buckler. Here a man fell, weltering in his blood; there another. Wounds began to stream crimson, and screams of agony rose from men wounded to death.

Conan grinned recklessly, white teeth flashing in his bronzed, heavy-featured face. The time for words was over. Although the years had taught him a measure of caution and responsibility, beneath his veneer of maturity there was still nothing that the grim barbarian relished more than a good free-for-all, and this looked to be the most glorious fight that had come his way in many a moon.

He leaped from the stairway, where he had stood, and came down on the nearest of Zarono's men. He bowled the man over and descended upon him with his boot-heels with such force as to snap the fellow's spine. Landing like a cat on all fours, Conan kicked the next man in the belly and thrust his sword between the ribs of the man who bent to assist his fallen comrade.

He plunged on, moving as lithely as a striking panther, despite his size, and cutting down the Zingarans like ripe wheat. He towered over the Zingarans, who were on the average a small people, the light swords with which they tried to parry the blows of his huge cutlass snapped at the impact, and men fell before him with a head or an arm shorn off. Behind him raged his buccaneers, swinging their cutlasses.

Most of the Zingarans on both sides were skilled swordsmen, scions of a people that had raised sword-play to a fine art. But Conan, though a barbarian born and bred, had made a life-long career of fighting and had studied it with the concentration of a connoisseur. While wintering in Kordava, he had employed his spare time in taking lessons in the refined Zingaran arts of swordplay from the great Master Valerio, whose fencing academy was reputed to turn out the finest swordsmen in several kingdoms.

So the down-at-heels young nobles of Villagro's following got a surprise when they swarmed in on Conan, expecting to feint the loutish barbarian out of position and skewer him as easily as impaling an apple with a dagger. Despite Conan's size and the weight of his blade, he easily thwarted their attacks. He countered their most subtle one-twos, doubles, binds, and coupes and stretched them, one after another, lifeless or gravely wounded on the bloody pave. Appalled, the young bluebloods fell back before this astounding giant who fought like a tiger and a tornado rolled into one.

Then a tall, slim figure in black velvet thrust its way through the press, and Black Zarono faced Conan sword to sword. Conan bled from several small cuts but wielded his blade as lightly as ever.

Zarono was no coward, but a ruthless, hard-bitten fighter. A dastard he was, but nobody had questioned his courage and lived. On the other hand, he was a shrewd, calculating man with an eye to the main chance. Had he thought more clearly, he would perhaps have refrained from facing Conan personally. But he was filled with a blazing hatred of Conan, who had thwarted him several times and whom he perversely blamed for the fall of his patron Villagro and the precarious state of his own fortunes. He had itched for revenge ever since that scuffle in the Nine Drawn Swords, when Conan's fist had all but knocked the head from his shoulders.

Zarono had no illusions about the gratitude that he could expect from Thoth-Amon, should the Stygian make good his claim to the Zingaran throne. All the posts of real power and wealth would doubtless go to Stygian priests of Set. But Thoth-Amon would probably condescend to allow Zarono some employment to live by; whereas, if the partisans of the old dynasty won, Zarono could look forward to nothing better than the ax and block.

Zarono's rapier – a heavier blade than most of the slender court swords wielded by Zarono's partisans – clanged against Conan's cutlass. Zarono made a dexterous pass at Conan, but the Cimmerian beat it off. Conan in turn feinted and aimed a fierce downward cut at Zarono's head; Zarono slipped to one side, and the cutlass skittered off his blade with a rasp of steel.

All around swirled the battle. More men had fallen, until the chamber had become a shambles. The numbers of Zarono's partisans began to tell. The loyalists were separated into two groups and driven back, one to the foot of the stairs down which Conan had come; the other, with the tottering old king in their midst, back into a corner.

And still Conan and Zarono fought on. Zarono began to realize that his lust for battle with his personal enemy had led him into an error. For, while his skill as a swordsman equaled Conan's, his arm did not have quite the Cimmerian's incredible strength and tireless dexterity. He began to tire, but fury and rancor kept him grimly at his task. He would slay the giant barbarian or die trying.

Meanwhile Thoth-Amon, imperturbable as ever, stepped down from the dais. Avoiding the knots of fighters, he walked calmly across the blood-wet, corpse-littered floor to where the Cobra Crown lay unheeded on the marble. Several times he passed within easy reach of one or another of Conan's partisans, but none ever sought to strike at him. It was as if he were invisible to them.

The fact was that, while they could see him plainly, he used his mental powers to deprive them of all will to harm him. So preoccupied was he with thus psychically guarding his own person that he had no attention left over to try to seize control of the minds of Conan and other leaders of the opposing faction. Nor could he, without his magical apparatus and without the quiet and solitude required for major magical works, perform any great thaumaturgies. Having discharged his green ray, he would not be able to use it again for hours.

Thoth-Amon indifferently passed the sprawled body of Menkara, slain by a chance thrust from an unknown hand. Reaching the Crown, the great Stygian stooped and picked it up. It was still hot to the touch, but Thoth-Amon grasped it firmly without sign of pain or damage. He turned it over, quickly examining it. Then, with a guttural curse, he tossed it aside as one would discard a useless bauble.

At that instant, another chorus of shouts came from above. The rest of Conan's crew, with Zeltran and Sigurd at their head, poured down the stairs, brandishing pikes and cutlasses. When Conan had set out with Ninus to the palace, he had sent Sigurd back to the ship, with instructions, obtained from Ninus, to enable the other Wastrels to follow him and to gain access to the palace by the secret tunnel known to Ninus.

These reinforcements instantly changed the aspect of the battle. The loyalists who had been driven back to the base of the stairs now pushed out again. The front of the Stygian party crumbled before the thrust. Conan and Zarono were borne along in the rush, losing contact.

Not yet resigned to giving up his battle with Conan, Zarono elbowed and struggled to keep his feet. As the press opened out, he felt a powerful grip on his sword arm. He tried to shake it off before he realized that it was Thoth-Amon who gripped him.

'It is time to cut our losses,' shouted the Stygian over the din. 'The Crown is ruined – burnt out.'

'Let me go!' cried Zarono angrily. 'We still have a good chance, and I'll kill that swine yet!'

'The gods have ordained that Conan shall win this time.'

'How do know you?'

Thoth-Amon shrugged. 'I know many things. I go; stay or follow, as you please.'

The Stygian turned away and started for the doorway. Zarono half-reluctantly followed him.

'Hold!' bellowed Conan's voice. 'You two dogs shan't get away so easily!'

Struggling out of a tangle of fighters, Conan rushed toward the departing pair, streaming blood from minor wounds and whirling his bloody cutlass.

Thoth-Amon raised an eyebrow. 'Barbarian, you begin to weary me.' The Stygian pointed the middle finger of his left hand – the one that bore a massive copper ring in the form of a serpent holding its tail in its mouth – toward a tapestry that hung between two of the narrow windows. *'N' ghokh-ghaa nafayak fthangug! Vgoh nyekh!'*

The tapestry seemed to come alive. It rippled, billowed, and tore loose from its attachments with a ripping sound. Like some colossal bat, it swooped out from the wall over the heads of the battlers. Arriving directly over Conan, it dropped straight down, enveloping him in its folds.

'Now hasten, if you would not be shortened by a head,' said Thoth-Amon to Zarono.

Seconds later, when Conan had struggled and slashed his way out from beneath the tapestry, Thoth-Amon and Zarono had vanished. All around, their followers, deserted by their leaders, were throwing down their weapons in surrender.

Cutlass in hand, Conan raced out the doorway and through the vestibule to the main entrance. He arrived to hear the galloping hoofbeats of the fugitives dwindling away to silence.

The dawn wind blew fresh and lusty. Salt spray rode upon it, and it stretched taut the booming sails of the *Wastrel* as she cleared the harbor of Kordava and pointed her prow to the open sea.

On the quarterdeck, newly cropped and shaven and clad in new gear, from plumed hat to shiny jackboots, Conan filled his lungs with a gusty sigh of contentment. Enough of these stinking magical spells, this battling with insubstantial shadows! Give him a stout ship and a crew of hearty cutthroats, a sword at his side, and a treasure to win, and he had all he wanted of the joys of the earth.

'By the teats of Ishtar and the privates of Nergal, shipmate, but I still think ye be stark, staring mad!' grumbled Sigurd the Vanr.

'Why? Because I wouldn't let Chabela marry me?' Conan grinned.

The red-bearded Northman nodded. 'She's a fine, round, bouncing lass, who'd bear you strong sons; and the throne of Zingara is yours for the asking. Surely, after all the excitement, old King Ferdrugo will not last much longer. Then the lass will inherit crown and kingdom and all!'

'I'll be no queen's consort, thank you,' growled Conan. 'I had my fill of that life in Gamburu, having no choice in the matter. And Nzinga was a lusty, strapping wench, not a silly, romantical child half my age. Besides, Ferdrugo may last longer than you think. Now that his wits are no longer befuddled by Stygian spells, he looks ten years younger and goes about his business in proper kingly fashion. The first thing he did was to annul that mad proclamation, abdicating and wedding Chabela to Thoth-Amon.

'As for Chabela – well, I like the child; I even love her in a fatherly sort of way. Betwixt you and me, I might even have taken up her offer, if I hadn't had an advance view of my fate.'

'How so?'

' 'Twas during the days following the battle, when my cuts were healing. I dined several times with the king and his daughter, and Chabela filled my ears with her plans for making me over. My speech, my dress, my table manners, my ideas of pleasure – all were to be changed. I was to become the perfect Zingaran gentleman, waving a scented handkerchief before my nose whilst I watched the royal ballet troupe go through its gyrations.

'Now, I may not be so wise as Godrigo, the king's pet philosopher; but I know what I like. Nay, Sigurd, I'll win myself a throne some day, Crom willing; but 'twill most likely be at the point of a sword, not as a wedding gift.

'Meanwhile, Ferdrugo has been generous to a fault. He gave me the Cobra Crown, which I have earning usury with Julio the goldsmith; that's where this new rigging and the new equipment for the lads came from.' Conan chuckled. 'Here I am, not yet forty, and already I'm becoming a penny-pinching money-grubber! I'd better be about the proper business of a buccaneer ere it's too late, and I turn into a potbellied miser.

'Kingdom-saving is no proper work for honest rogues like us, and doubtless there'll be plenty of fat-bellied merchantmen sailing from Argos and Shem. Leave off your mooning over my refusal of the offer of a moonstruck girl, and let's think of business. Come look at the charts in my cabin.' He raised his voice. 'Master Zeltran! Join us in the cabin, if you please.'

Conan strode away. For a moment, the big red-beard stared after him open-mouthed. Then he lifted his hands in a shrug of despair and followed his captain.

'By Llyr's green beard and Thor's hammer,' he groaned, 'but there be just no arguing with a Cimmerian!

The rigging creaked, the bow wave soughed, and the gulls squealed as the *Wastrel* sailed southward, bearing Conan to new adventures.